THE FLUTTERING

Something terrifying has started happening in Eggerton. People are turning up drained of blood and very, very dead. Have vampire bats started attacking humans? If so, then who's delivering the hammer-blow that finally kills the victims? For Detective Inspector Jack Sears it's a mystery that not even virologist Doctor Christopher Deacon can fathom. But then the police get lucky. Against all the odds one of the victims survives. But strangely enough, that's when things go from bad to worse . . .

DAVID WHITEHEAD

THE FLUTTERING

Complete and Unabridged

LINFORD
Leicester

First published in Great Britain in 2008

First Linford Edition
published 2009

British Library CIP Data

Whitehead, David, *1958* –
    The fluttering - - (Linford mystery library)
    1. Serial murder investigation- -Fiction.
    2. Detective and mystery stories.
    3. Large type books.
    I. Title II. Series
    823.9′14–dc22

    ISBN 978–1–84782–829–3

Published by
F. A. Thorpe (Publishing)
Anstey, Leicestershire

Set by Words & Graphics Ltd.
Anstey, Leicestershire
Printed and bound in Great Britain by
T. J. International Ltd., Padstow, Cornwall
This book is printed on acid-free paper

For Dad

1

Perching more than sitting on the edge of the armchair, Terry Marsh went over it again for what seemed like the thousandth time. But no matter how hard he tried, he still couldn't quite grasp the enormity of what had happened.

Of what he'd *done*.

Terry had started the day as an ordinary working stiff.

He'd ended it as a murderer.

Again he ran trembling fingers up through his spiky blond crew-cut, tears returning unbidden to his tormented brown eyes. No. It was no good. Try as he might, he *still* couldn't believe that he'd actually done it.

But as denial gradually faded, acceptance finally began to set in. He *had* killed her. He *had!* It was done, and God help him, there was no undoing it.

The question now was, what was he going to *do* about it?

He got up, never once taking his eyes off the body on the floor, and took a quick, restless turn around the small living room, alternately wringing, then flexing, his big, bruised hands.

He was a stocky thirty year-old with a square face and a ruddy complexion that was now drained of colour. Poorly educated and easily confused, he'd always been a bit slow when it came to thinking and making decisions. Sue had usually done all the thinking for them both. But of course, Sue wasn't here anymore.

It came to him then that he should call the police. That was it. If he owned up to it, told them it was all a mistake, an accident, they'd go easy on him, right?

Right?

But even if they went easy on him, he was still looking at a lengthy prison sentence, and he was by no means sure that he could handle that.

He fell more than sank onto the sofa, playing things back through his mind and wondering how the police would see it. For a start, they'd want to know how it all began, and that in itself brought him up sharp.

How *had* it all begun, anyway?

He guessed it had started with Baby.

That's what they'd always called him, or her. *Baby*. Because he, or she, had never really gotten the chance to *become* a he or a she.

Baby had died at twelve weeks, when Sue miscarried. That had been six months earlier.

Before Baby, their seven-year marriage had been a rocky affair at best. He worked as a warehouseman, she as a checkout operator at the local supermarket, both of them stuck in menial, dead-end jobs at minimum wage. She had quickly grown sick of the grotty second-floor council flat they lived in, wanted to better herself and get a foot on the property ladder. He, by contrast, was a plodder who had no desire to climb any higher.

Sometimes she must have wondered why they'd ever bothered to get married in the first place. He knew there were plenty of times when *he* had.

They'd first met when he was fifteen and she was fourteen. Always shy around girls, Terry had quickly clung to her with an obsessive kind of desperation, always secretly afraid that someone else would come along and steal her away from him. And Sue, basking in his puppy-like adoration, had been happy to encourage his behaviour.

But life in the real world had started to bite as soon as they got married. For a start, the home Sue had always dreamed of turned out to be a dismal two-bedroom flat on Eggerton's notorious Crowley Estate. And there were always bills to pay, and never enough money with which to pay them.

Gradually, this seemingly endless procession of demands and disappointments had driven a wedge between them, and after a while they'd taken to scowling rather than smiling at each other, snapping rather than speaking, and each had gone his or her own short-tempered way and more or less left the other to it.

Of course, there were still the occasional good times, and about four weeks after one such, Sue — small, slim Sue, with her oval face topped by short, butter-coloured hair that was jet black at the roots — announced that she was pregnant.

At last they had something upon which they could both agree — that the news was fantastic.

Sue in particular had been over the moon. Ever since her mother had died two years earlier, she'd had no family that she really knew, only Terry. But with Baby all that would change.

Terry sobbed harder now, as he recalled that happy time, for as dense as he was, it hadn't taken him long to realise that Baby was the one thing that had always been missing from their relation-ship. Baby was going to be the answer to all their problems, the cement that finally bound them both together.

Baby had taken over their lives after that, and throwing their usual financial caution to the wind, they'd been unable to resist buying bath toys, a nursing pillow and snuggle blankets, bibs, romper suits (always in neutral colours, of course, like white, cream or lemon), even a thermometer.

But that had been early on. Before Sue had started cramping and bleeding.

Oh God, what a time *that* had been, he remembered. The fear he'd known then, when Sue's grave-faced doctor had requested an ultra-sound to make sure everything was still all right . . . and then the giddying rush of relief when they found out that Baby was still there and still doing fine —

But then the bleeding had started again, and this time the pain that accompanied it had buckled Sue up. She'd had to be rushed to the hospital by ambulance, where a doctor who looked too young to *be* a doctor eventually mumbled something apologetic about chromosomal abnormalities, and Baby not being viable.

Viable!

What he meant was that Baby — who couldn't even tip the scales at half a kilo — wasn't worth the effort of saving.

Yes. That was where it had all gone wrong.

In the weeks that followed, they'd been *empty*, somehow. Just two drained, joyless people going through the motions. The old enmities had started to resurface, the angry flare-ups, the sarcastic sideswipes, the long silences.

And then Sue suggested they try again.

He'd immediately backed off from her, unwilling to go through that particular kind of agony all over again. Besides — and he hated to admit it, even to himself — he couldn't get that phrase, *chromosomal abnormalities*, out of his mind.

What did it mean? Had Baby been some sort of freak that was better off dead? And what if those same abnormalities affected Baby 2, and he or she *survived*? What would their life be like then, looking after some drooling half-monster?

It was stupid, of course. Of *course* it was stupid. But he hadn't been capable of thinking properly since the miscarriage, and once the idea got lodged in his brain there was no shifting it.

The more she wanted to try for another

baby, the less willing he was to oblige her. Sometimes it was easier to stay up late into the night, telling her there was something on TV he wanted to watch, or to feign deep sleep every time he heard the mattress shift under her slender weight as she reached for him.

He didn't fool her for a moment, though. She knew he was trying to avoid her. And the longer it went on, the harder it became for both of them.

One night she fixed him with a steady look and said, right out of the blue, 'Don't you want me any more?'

There was anger in her wide-spaced hazel eyes, a challenging pout to her thin lips.

'What's that supposed to mean?' he asked.

He knew perfectly well what it meant, of course.

She tried a more direct approach. 'Are you getting it from someone else?'

'No, I'm *not*,' he replied more firmly. 'What's got into you, anyway? Are you trying to pick a fight or something?'

'No,' she said. 'But I think *you* are.'

Afterwards, he thought about what she'd said. *Are you getting it from someone else?* It wasn't like her to be quite so crude. But she had a point. He was only human, after all. And if he didn't get it from somewhere, and soon, he was liable to burst.

On his tea-break at work one morning, he was leafing through the local paper when he happened to spot an ad in the *Personal* column, apparently placed by a bored housewife called Celia, who said she was available for discreet fun at any time.

For some reason the advert, and more specifically the prospect of actually *answering* it, tantalised him. So, that same lunch-time, he found a quiet bench in the nearby shopping precinct and thumbed Celia's number into his mobile phone.

It rang three times before a woman's voice said, 'Hello, this is Celia.'

With pounding heart, Terry said, 'Oh, uh, I . . . '

'Leave a message after the tone, and I'll call you back.'

The moment he realised that he'd been listening to a recorded message his nerve deserted him altogether, and he quickly rang off.

For Terry, it was suddenly like coming out of a dream. What was he thinking of, anyway? Bored housewife! What she'd really meant was *prostitute*. And though he'd never been what you might call a prude, the idea that he could even *think* about being unfaithful to Sue finally shocked him out of the haze in which he'd been trapped ever since Baby had died.

That evening he didn't go straight home from work. He stopped off at the pub, bought himself a Leffe and sat in a shadowy corner, determined to do some serious thinking. He thought about how stupid and selfish he'd been over the past few months, about what he'd stood to lose, and by the time he'd finished his second pint, he'd reached an important decision.

He hurried out into the street and caught the bus home.

The Crowley Estate was a maze of

narrow, car- and skip-choked streets hemmed in by grey, graffiti-stained blocks of flats and grubby little bed-sits reserved for the care-in-the-community brigade.

It was funny how he'd never really seen it that way before. But now, everywhere he looked, he saw reasons to move: gangs of kids loitering on corners, surveying the world from under baseball caps and hoodies: burned-out wrecks of cars standing up on blocks: overgrown gardens littered with old settees and discarded fridges: mindless music pounding from every open window.

Sue was waiting for him when he got in, and she didn't look especially happy. It wasn't late, just a little after eight, but he suddenly realised that he'd been so wrapped up in himself that he hadn't thought to call and let her know where he was.

'Sue,' he said, taking off his old denim jacket and throwing it over the arm of a chair. 'I've got something to say.'

And he'd been rehearsing it all the way home. *I'm sorry. I haven't been thinking straight since we lost Baby. I know I've hurt you, I know I don't deserve another chance, but if you'll let me I'll do better this time, I promise. As for trying for another baby, yes, yes, if that's what you want —*

Before he could say anything at all, however, Sue said, '*I've* got something to say, as well.'

Not picking up on the brittle edge to her voice, he said eagerly, 'All right. You go first, then.'

She did. She said, 'I want you to pack your bags and go, Terry, and I want you to do it now, tonight.'

As slow as ever to catch on, he said stupidly, 'What?'

'It's over, Terry. It's been over a long time now. I think it's about time we made it official.'

'But — I don't — '

'There's someone else,' she said. 'And I'm having his baby.'

He thought, *Baby?* And he said, foolishly, 'Baby?'

She could see by the look on his face that he needed help, so she spelled it out for him, her voice low, shaky.

'I wanted a baby, Terry. I needed to feel loved and wanted. But you cut yourself off from me. So I went elsewhere, and I was lucky enough to find all the love I could ever need.'

Incredibly, he was still confused. 'Who is he?' he managed to croak at last.

'No one *you'd* know.'

'How long has this been going on, then?'

'*Months*,' she replied.

And that was when it hit him. All this time he'd been so wrapped up in himself that he hadn't even realised what had been going on right under his nose.

He stared at her, and the disappointment he felt fuelled an uncharacteristic rage within him. *All this time*, he thought again. No wonder she hadn't bothered going back to work after they lost Baby. She'd been too busy entertaining her fancy man!

The idea of them being here while he was at work, the thought of all the secrets they must have shared and the things they'd done . . .

And now here she was, telling him, *I'm having his baby*.

13

'You bitch,' he whispered.

Just for a moment then she looked a little nervous. 'Just get your stuff and go,' she said.

'To make room for the new bloke, you mean?' he replied, his voice rising. 'Oh, no! If anyone's moving out, it's *you!* Go on, get your stuff and bugger off out of it!'

'Terry, look, I — '

'*Go on, bugger off!*' he yelled.

She really should have gone.

She didn't.

She said, 'There's no need to be — '

And by then it was too late.

He grabbed her by the arms in one adrenalin-fuelled blur, stared her straight in the face and screamed '*Bugger off!*' with such vehemence that spittle flew off his lips. '*And take your little bastard with you!*'

She reacted to that. She said something, he didn't quite catch what it was, and she slapped him, hard.

That did it.

All at once everything ceased to exist except Sue and the pain she had caused him. He hit her back, she screamed and tried to claw his face, but he batted her hands aside and hit her again, again, again, and each blow carried just a *little* more force than the one before it.

He had one brief image of Sue's oval face, reddening with fresh bruises, and of her eyes, large now, and scared. Her hair was wild. She was saying something, trying to, but now that he'd started hitting her, he just couldn't seem to stop . . .

She grabbed him. They wrestled for a moment. His feet tangled with hers and they nearly went over, but not quite.

He punched her, left, right, left, right, heard the harsh, wet slapping sounds each blow made, the small, scared cries each strike drew from her. She was begging now, he realized dimly, but there was no longer any clemency in him, only rage, and pain, and disappointment.

Some incalculable time later he stopped punching her. She was sprawled on the floor and he was straddling her, gasping for air, sweating hard, his trembling arms too heavy to lift any more.

He blinked down at her. Her face was so bruised and bloodied and swollen that he saw nothing there that he recognised.

'. . . Sue . . . ?' he said uncertainly, his voice that of a lost little boy.

She lay still and quiet beneath him.

She was dead.

2

Terry's eyes shuttled back toward the body. Thinking about it, he didn't believe the police would show him any more mercy than he'd shown Sue. But what else could he do? He had to come clean ... *hadn't* he? Of course he had to! Sooner or later she'd be missed, she was bound to be.

But even as he thought it, a little voice in his head asked him, *Why?*

It was, he thought, a very good question.

Sue had no relations to speak of, and no real friends. The only person likely to wonder where she'd gone would be her fancy man, whoever he was. But would he risk asking her husband what had become of her? Terry doubted it. He might go to the police, of course. It all depended on just how strongly he felt about her. But what if he *didn't?*

The evening wore on. Terry continued

to stare at the body and try to decide what to do about the mess in which he now found himself.

And because he still wasn't thinking clearly, because the two pints of Leffe he'd consumed earlier had left him ever-so-slightly drunk, he began to wonder if he really *could* get away with murder.

The more he thought about it, the more he realised how anonymous he and Sue had always been. There'd be no one to really *miss* Sue. But everything hinged on his being able to get rid of the body.

He was over the shock now, more or less. And every time he felt the painful stirrings of remorse, he remembered what had led up to the fight in the first place, what she'd been doing all these weeks and months behind his back, and that helped him stay focused. Self-preservation was the order of the day now. That, and damage limitation. But it would take some thinking about, and thinking had never been Terry's strongest suit.

He needed to get rid of the body. But where? Where would it never be found?

He puzzled over the matter long into the night, but the answer continued to elude him.

Suddenly overwhelmed by a terrible cocktail of anxiety and desperation, he sprang up and crossed to the living room window. In the moonlight, the estate resembled a slumbering war zone.

But beyond the estate lay Chapel Cut.

It was a narrow, disused canal that ended at Monk's Tunnel, a bridge that had been bombed by the Germans during World War II and never rebuilt.

Now the place was a fly-tipper's dream. Overhung by screening trees, its weedy banks were knee-deep in all kinds of rubbish. The water itself was green and oily, home to shopping trolleys and bicycle frames and Christ alone knew what else.

It was also deep — fifteen feet, he'd heard once, after one of the local kids had drowned in it.

In his disordered mind, it seemed like the perfect spot.

But he cautioned himself against doing anything rash — as if he hadn't *already* done anything rash that evening. He had to think about this first, plan exactly how he was going to do it.

First thing he had to do was take a closer look at the area, make sure the plan was . . . oh, what was the word again?

That was it.

Viable.

He turned, grabbed his jacket, took one more look at Sue and thought, *Oh, Christ* . . . His eyes screwed shut and his fists folded up and he thought for a minute that his head was going to explode.

Then the moment passed and he left the room, switching off the light as he did so, and plunging Sue — what was left of her — into darkness.

★ ★ ★

As he hurried through the poorly-lit estate, which was quieter now, and largely deserted because of the lateness of the hour, he started thinking again and tried not to. He just couldn't face what he'd done, he really *couldn't* face it, and not just because of what he'd done to Sue, but because of what he'd done to the baby she'd said she was carrying.

Anyway, he should be concentrating more on the practicalities now. Like how he was going to get Sue down here without anyone seeing him. She wasn't big, a size eight, no weight in her at all. But he could hardly just throw her across his shoulder and carry her down to Chapel Cut.

He'd have to think about that.

The estate fell behind him, and with a quick, self-conscious glance around, he crossed a silent road that was bathed sickly yellow beneath the glow of sodium vapour streetlights. On the far side lay the inky darkness of the Cut, a shunned, neglected area around which even the local kids seldom played anymore.

He found a section of chain-link fence that had been partially torn loose and fumbled his way down the weed-choked embankment towards the dark, moon-silvered slash of the canal itself. The June night was clear, quiet, humid.

He stumbled on for a few hundred metres, searching for the right place and wishing he'd thought to fetch a torch with him, until at length he could just about discern the jagged silhouette of Monk's Tunnel in the near distance, a black half-oval that ended in several tons of brick, cement and twisted steel.

From here he would be hidden from any prying eyes. He could slide Sue's lifeless body into the greasy water with no fear of being seen, and she would sink gracefully to the bottom, and if he was lucky, if he was *really* lucky, she would never be seen again.

He was so wrapped up in the thought that he suddenly tripped and tumbled forward onto his hands and knees, scraping all four on rough ground strewn with broken glass.

'*Shit!*'

The curse came out louder than he'd intended, and it sounded even louder still in the near-absolute stillness of the night. Although he wanted to check his palms for cuts, he forced himself to remain still, convinced that he'd alerted everyone within a thousand miles to his presence there in the lonely gloom.

After a long moment he allowed himself to start breathing again, held his hands up and examined them in the moonlight. Bugger it — he'd cut his right palm. He'd have to clean that when he got back home.

He looked behind him. As near as he could tell, he'd tripped over a pile of broken Thermalite blocks.

Thermalite blocks, he thought, standing up again. *I can weigh the body down with those.*

And it was then, as an electric shock of horror washed through him at the matter-of-fact way he was going about this thing, that he suddenly came rushing back to his senses.

What the hell am I doing? he asked himself. *Isn't it enough that I killed her? That I killed the baby inside her? What the hell am I thinking about, coming here, doing this?*

Shaken to the core now, he slowly wrapped a handkerchief around his hand and told himself to be a man and own up to what he'd done. That's what he should have done all along, what he *would* have done, if she hadn't hurt him so much and he hadn't been half-cut.

The decision made, and a heavy weight lifted, he was just turning for home when a quick, fluttering rush of sound caught his attention, and as he glanced back toward Monk's Tunnel he saw a flock of what he took to be birds rising from its gaping black mouth into the star-speckled sky above.

He had a vague idea that they might be starlings. He'd seen them on television once, the way they congregated at dusk, swirling like a restless black wave that swept back and forth, back and forth, before section after section gradually peeled away to swoop down into their roosting spots.

But then it occurred to him that this wasn't dusk, it was late night, and that these birds weren't descending, they were corkscrewing ever higher in a sleek, chattering funnel, black and restless against the dark blue of the night sky.

He tired of them then, and was about to retrace his steps back to the flat when he realised that the bird-thing at the head of the spiral had suddenly tipped over onto one side and was beginning to dive back to earth.

He thought vaguely, *If I didn't know better . . .*

And then, following their leader, the birds behind the first also began to tilt wing-over and plunge earthward in its wake.

If I didn't know better . . . I'd say they've seen me.

That they're coming this way.

It was a ridiculous notion. But an uneasiness that had nothing to do with the events of the evening suddenly began to stir within Terry, and as fluttering shape after fluttering shape seemed to reach the pinnacle of its ascent and then fall away to begin a fully-controlled plummet back to earth, he turned again and started hurrying along the uneven canal bank.

He heard it again then, above the rough, irregular sawing of his own breath, that rapid fluttering sound, and was sure it wasn't just his imagination. It was a quick, leathery tattoo, and it was growing louder —

In the next moment something dark and heavy skimmed across the top of his head, brushing at his spiky blond hair, and he couldn't help it, he gave a sort of startled yelp.

Then the thing, whatever it was, was gone, and he was jogging even faster, with the knee-high weeds rustling dryly around him, and a clammy sweat breaking on his —

Again something dove low and scratch-scraped at his head. He reached up, tried to swat the thing away, but it was already gone, a flittering, fluttering shadow in the night.

He took another flurry of steps, caught one foot on something, maybe a spill of trailing bindweed, and toppled forward with another cry spilling from his lips.

The ground came up and hit him, hard. Lights popped inside his head and he had to fight to draw breath back into his suddenly-emptied lungs.

He thrust back to his hands and knees, but before he could get his feet under him again something heavy whacked him between the shoulder-blades and sent

26

him sprawling back onto his face.

He rolled, swatting violently at the empty air, stopped when he realised that there was nothing there to swat, no further sign of the birds or bats or whatever they were.

Then he glanced down at the ground just beyond his feet, and screamed.

What looked like a million bats had landed among the weeds and were hopping, leaping and scuttling towards him in a swarming, squeaking, wing-fluttering *torrent*, and they were big buggers, bigger than any birds or bats he'd ever seen before —

Terry yelled again, tried to roll over and get his legs back under him, but it was already too late.

Bats leapt up to hit him in the face, sink their claws into his hair, latch onto his ears with razor-sharp canines and incisors, and he went down again, rolling frantically to try and dislodge them.

But there were even more of them now, settling on his face, smothering him, landing on his chest in such numbers that he could barely move beneath their weight.

He managed to rip one of the smaller bats from his face and hurl it aside, but almost immediately its place was taken by two more. He opened his mouth to voice another scream but as soon as his lips parted yet another bat shoved its head inside and sunk its teeth into his tongue.

He rolled first one way, then the other, but his movements were even more restricted now because he was covered in them, literally *covered* in them, and they were a heaving, seething mass that chattered incessantly as they worried at his flesh, clawing, gnawing, nipping, ripping —

He managed to tear another bat away from his right eye. The bat took part of his eyelid with it. He wanted to scream but the best he could manage was a low, feverish, '*Help me . . . somebody, pl-please help me . . .*'

A moment later, as one of the crawling bats lost its grip on his nose and slipped sideways off his face, something wonderful seemed to happen.

As incredible as it seemed, he actually spotted someone making their way towards him from the direction of Monk's Tunnel.

He could hardly believe his luck. He was saved!

As the poorly-defined silhouette of a man of about average height or maybe a little less rapidly drew closer, Terry felt a pitiful rush of gratitude.

'*Help me!*' he gurgled beneath the press of fluttering bats.

And, amazingly, the newcomer *did* help him.

He brought up the hammer he'd been clutching in his right hand and smashed Terry's brains in.

3

'All right, Frank,' said Detective Inspector Jack Sears, climbing out of his maroon Audi and shutting the driver's-side door behind him. 'What have we got?'

It was a little after seven o'clock on Saturday morning, and Chapel Cut looked even more depressing than usual. Or maybe it was just the cynical mood in which Sears existed these days that made it seem that way.

A crowd of onlookers — mostly fat women with tattooed arms and thin men in baseball caps, with grubby-faced kids weaving bicycles in and out between them — had already gathered on the other side of the road, drawn to the area by the arrival of the Incident Support Units.

Detective Sergeant Frank Ryan, a tall, skinny man with a long neck and a restless Adam's apple, said briskly, 'Bloke out walking his dog about an hour ago, does the same walk at the same time every day. This morning the dog ran off ahead, started sniffing at something in the long grass, then suddenly backed away and started howling. The geezer reckons he'd never seen the dog act that way before, so he went over to see what all the fuss was about, and found a body.'

'Male or female?'

'Male.'

'Do we have any ID yet?'

'Security pass in his jacket pocket identifies him as Terence William Marsh,' supplied Ryan. 'Local man.'

'Any previous?'

'Nothing.'

'All right. Let's have a look.'

Sears stepped over a section of buckled chain-link fence and together he and Ryan picked a cautious path down the rubbish-littered embankment and onto the canal bank itself.

Blue and white POLICE LINE DO NOT CROSS tape had already been used to define three distinct perimeters, one to keep the public at bay, the second to act as a sort of buffer zone where the investigation could be coordinated, and the third to isolate the crime-scene itself. About fifty metres away, a small white tent with a pitched yellow roof had been erected over the body.

'What do we know about the deceased?' asked Sears, a tall, compact man just past his mid-forties, with fine brown hair and a square face that showed evidence of a youth spent sparring in amateur boxing clubs.

'Not much. Worked as a warehouseman down at Bell and Harmon.'

'The carpet and bedding people?'

'That's the one.'

'And you say he's a local man?'

'Lived just over there, on the Crowley Estate.'

'Poor sod. Better inform the next-of-kin, then, before word gets out.'

'I'll get Claire Jarvis onto it right away,' nodded Ryan, naming the unit's Family Liaison Officer. He hurried away, leaving Sears to pick the rest of the way to the tent alone.

The canal bank was bustling with activity. Assistant scene-of-crime officers dressed in protective clothing were photographing or sketching the area, or conducting visual and shoulder-to-shoulder fingertip searches. A badly shaken man in his early sixties, with a shaggy black Collie sitting patiently beside him, was giving his statement to a WPC, who was scribbling notes onto a clipboard pad.

David Schofield, the pathologist, was just withdrawing a thermometer probe from under the dead man's right armpit when Sears entered the tent. The Senior SOCO, John Richards, was hovering nearby, waiting for Schofield to finish so that he could begin his own forensic examination of the body and its immediate environs.

Both men looked around as Sears came in, tugged at the crease of his grey suit trousers and dropped to his haunches beside the body.

The dead man was sprawled on his back. He was about thirty, heavy-set and with short blond hair. His eyes were still open. Beneath the vitreous humour — the thin, near-transparent film of jelly that covered them — they were the colour of chocolate. He wore jeans, a tee-shirt and a denim jacket.

The left side of his head had been caved in by what appeared to be a single blow.

The most startling thing about him, however, was his complexion. Sears had seen plenty of bodies in his time, but few as pallid as this one. Terry Marsh's face was as pale as paper, except for the puffed, tiny blue contusions that were visible around a series of small, slit-like incisions that covered his face, hands, ears and neck.

'Morning all,' Sears greeted perfunctorily. 'What have we got, Dave?'

Schofield, an overweight man in his early fifties, finished writing something down with an expensive fountain pen, then said, 'A right old puzzle, I'm afraid.'

'Do tell.'

'This man's been more or less desanguinated,' announced Schofield. 'Hardly any blood left in him at all.'

Sears considered that. 'Should we be surprised?' he asked after a moment. 'He must have lost a fair bit from the head-wound alone.'

'Certainly,' agreed the pathologist. 'But

that wouldn't account for *all* of it. As you know, blood doesn't so much *flow* after death as *ooze*. Within half an hour, gravity ensures that it pools at the lowest point in the body. And yet, as near as I can tell at the moment, this man's veins are virtually *empty*.'

'Could he have haemorrhaged?'

'I haven't found anything to suggest it.'

'Was he dehydrated?'

'No. And before you ask, there's nothing to indicate that he'd been drinking to excess, either.'

'Then where did it all go?'

Schofield arched one eyebrow. 'You're the detective,' he said.

Sears' brief smile stirred the neatly-trimmed moustache he wore above his thin, sober mouth. '*Touché*. How did he die, then? From the head-wound, presumably?'

'I'll know more when I open him up, but for now I'd have to say loss of blood on a *massive* scale.'

As Ryan entered the tent behind him, Sears asked, 'Time of death?'

Schofield pursed his fleshy lips. The

product of one too many pub lunches, he had a heavy, ruddy face and short, prematurely white hair. 'About midnight. Maybe a little after.'

'How do you read it, Frank?'

Ryan said, 'Look at the state of his knuckles, Guv. He obviously had a run-in with someone and came off worst.'

Sears had already noticed the condition of the dead man's hands. The knuckles were skinned, a little swollen and bruised, and it appeared that he'd tried to bind some sort of wound on his right palm. But there was one problem with Ryan's suggestion.

'These marks,' he said, indicating the corpse's face. 'They're not consistent with any kind of fist fight. What are they, anyway, Dave?'

'Punctures of some sort.'

'Insect bites?' prodded Sears. 'Rats?'

'I don't think so.'

Sears studied the ground around the body. 'He was definitely killed here?'

Speaking for the first time, John Richards said, 'Yes. Everywhere you look, you can see signs of a struggle.'

'But precious little blood?'

'Hardly a drop.'

'What happened to his eyelid? Looks like it's been torn off.'

Schofield shrugged. 'That *could* be the work of rats. I'll know more, later.'

'All right,' said Sears, pushing back to his feet, 'we'll leave you to it, then. But let me have whatever you can ASAP, will you?'

'As always, Jack.'

Outside again, Sears glanced at Ryan and said, 'He was a warehouseman, you say?'

Ryan nodded.

'He didn't handle chemicals at all?'

'I wouldn't have thought so. Why?'

'Didn't you notice that smell around the body? A bit like ammonia?'

'Smelled more like fox piss to me.'

Sears shrugged. 'You could be right. There's probably plenty of 'em around here.'

He ran his penetrating brown eyes over the area. It was a squalid section of a squalid area, where squalid things like this had a habit of happening with depressing regularity. Sensing Ryan watching him, he gestured to the tower blocks opposite and said, 'Better get some uniforms up there soon as you can. You never know, someone might have seen or heard something around midnight last night.'

'Will do.'

'And see what you can find out about Marsh himself. What kind of neighbour was he? Did he have any problems at work, or home? Did he owe anyone money?'

Ryan nodded. 'Anything else?'

'Yes,' said Sears, pointing toward the overgrown mouth of Monk's Tunnel. 'I want to know what's in there.'

'I'll fix it,' said Ryan.

He was about to say more when one of the uniforms up at street level suddenly called down, '*Skipper!*' and gestured for him to come up at the double.

'Won't be a minute, Guv,' said Ryan, and went jogging off to see what the problem was.

For a few seconds Sears watched him go. Then, shoving his hands deep into his trouser pockets, he wandered to the edge of the bank and stared moodily into the dark, greasy water, wondering what Stephanie had planned for the weekend. Nothing that involved him, that was for sure.

Then again, why should it? A year had passed, and she'd moved on.

He hadn't, though. He hadn't been *able* to.

Once upon a time he'd been a husband and a father and, latterly, a grandfather. But now Stephanie was gone, Charlie was gone, and he was and always would be a complete stranger to young Andrew.

He wasn't sure what hurt more.

He heard Ryan come hurrying back then, and tried to shrug off his dark mood. When he was near enough, Ryan said breathlessly, 'Talk about it never rains but it pours.'

'What's that supposed to mean?'

'I just got word from Claire Jarvis,' said Ryan. 'She went round to inform Marsh's next-of-kin, but couldn't get any reply.'

'So?'

'Well, she was just about to leave again when the next-door neighbour came out and said she'd heard raised voices in the flat last night, like Marsh and his wife were having a right old bust-up. Claire got a bad feeling about it and took the decision to call in some back-up. She and a couple of uniforms entered the flat by force . . . and get this.'

'They found Marsh's widow on the living room floor, beaten to death.'

★ ★ ★

The preliminary report came in a little after four o'clock that afternoon. Sears scanned it quickly, but if he was hoping it would give him something to go on, he was to be disappointed. So far, Terry Marsh's killer hadn't left anything behind him except question marks.

Forensics hadn't turned up anything specific, and door-to-door inquiries had yielded nothing of particular relevance. There were no decent boot or shoe prints at the crime-scene, no tyre prints nearby, and the clothes of the victim had failed to yield any prints that couldn't be accounted for.

Terry Marsh himself appeared to have

been a man of good character, who kept himself to himself and was liked by neighbours and workmates both.

And yet he'd beaten his wife to death the previous evening. Traces of Marsh's skin found in Sue Marsh's wounds proved that beyond all doubt.

Which left Sears with quite a conundrum.

For a start, why had the couple argued in the first place? What had Marsh been doing down by the canal approximately four hours after killing his wife? Contemplating suicide, perhaps? Or looking for somewhere to dump the body? And who had ended up killing him, and why?

He knew better than to assume that the second murder was a consequence of the first, but it was certainly something to think about.

According to David Schofield's report, Terry Marsh had been desanguinated. Loss of blood had resulted in multiple organ failure, leading to brain damage and coma. In other words, the poor bastard would've died even if someone hadn't bashed his brains in first.

The majority of the puncture wounds, now confirmed as bites, had been centred on the trachea, and for the most part followed the lines of the common carotid artery and the external jugular vein. The bites were tentatively identified as being those of a bat.

That at least tied in with what scene-of-crime officers had found at Monk's Tunnel. Apparently, there was some evidence to suggest that a small, cleared, cave-like area at its farthest end, which was almost invisible from the entrance itself, had recently been used as some sort of nest or roost. But for *what?*

'What do you make of it?' Sears called, sitting back in his chair and interlacing his fingers over his barely discernable paunch.

Ryan, busy with paperwork at his own desk outside, glanced up, then got up and came to lean in the doorway. 'Marsh and his wife argue,' he said. 'Marsh beats her to death, then goes out to cool off or decide what to do about it. Someone else goes after him, maybe another family member or a friend we haven't traced yet, beats his brains in, then legs it. Afterwards, the bats roosting in the tunnel are attracted to the body by the smell of all that lovely blood. I remember seeing something on telly once, where they said bats have a highly-developed sense of smell.'

'I like it,' said Sears, who'd been thinking along the same lines. 'The only trouble is, according to the autopsy report, the bats got to the buffet *before* the victim got his head smashed in.'

Ryan frowned. 'Then that would imply that the killer and the bats are somehow connected.'

'Maybe they *are*.'

'So what's our man doing with a bunch of trained bats?'

Sears gave him a sharp look. '*Can* you train bats?'

'God knows.'

'Well, we need to find out.' He thought quickly. 'I want every zoo and research establishment within a radius of, say, fifty miles checked out. Have they lost any bats recently? Have a word with all the pest control companies as well. I know you can't handle bats without a license, but you never know, someone might have reported a problem. But keep it low-key, Frank. The papers'll have a field day if they get hold of this.'

'I'll get right onto it,' said Ryan.

'And get me a bat man while you're about it,' added Sears. 'Someone who actually knows what he's talking about.'

Ryan was about to turn away when he suddenly hesitated. 'What about Robin?' he asked.

'Who's Robin, when he's at home?'

Ryan grinned. 'I just thought, you know, if I can't get Batman, can we make do with Robin?'

Sears threw him a withering look. 'Do me a favour, Frank,' he said. 'Don't give up your day job.'

4

Ronnie Spurgeon had never been known for his patience.

At the age of seven he'd been diagnosed with Attention Deficit Hyperactivity Disorder and his doctor had prescribed Ritalin, but all that had done was increase his moods and stop him from sleeping.

When his patience was likely to be rewarded, however, Ronnie could find surprising reserves of the stuff.

Like now, for example.

It was a little after ten o'clock on Saturday night, and he'd been waiting in the darkened shop doorway for about half an hour. Traffic along the normally-busy Culshaw Road was finally beginning to tail off, and beyond the streetlamps, the sky was gradually turning a deeper, darker blue.

Ronnie drew on his cigarette. For the briefest moment, the tip glowed bright orange, then dimmed again. Getting irritable now, he shifted his weight from one foot to the other — not that there was all that much weight to shift. Seventeen year-old Ronnie was as thin as a rail, and his over-large hooded sweater and baggy jeans served only to make him appear even more emaciated.

He blew smoke in a quick, nervy gesture, took a pace forward, glanced left, then right, then backed into the shadows again.

In the gloom he looked more like a skeleton than anything else, his nose long, his cheeks hollow, his mouth thin, his eyes, above his pronounced cheekbones, a sunken, pale blue glaze.

He did some more weight-shifting, threw the cigarette to the ground, stepped it out with the sole of one trainer, then stuffed his hands into his pockets.

Ronnie Spurgeon was very much a product of his times. His mother had been sixteen when she'd given birth to him, and had often taken great delight in telling him she had no clear idea just who his father had been. A diet of junk food and neglect had made him self-sufficient, after a fashion. But it had also made him lazy and indifferent to the world around him.

Excluded from school for a string of misdemeanors, he'd been able to indulge his two great passions, stealing and drinking, on a more or less full-time basis. His addiction to computer games — the really *good* ones, that was, the ones with plenty of blood and guts in them — had further distanced him from his stunted emotions.

Unemployed and unemployable, barely able to read and write and even less interested in trying to rectify the situation, he was content to drift through life like the wild animal he was, a creature of pure, blind instinct, entirely unencumbered by conscience.

Unable to switch off his racing, medication-soaked mind, he stayed up late into the night, *every* night, and slept late into the following day, *every* day. His mood swings, which lurched from feelings of great self-importance to those of extreme self-loathing, made him impossible to live with.

He leaned against the shop doorway, shoved back onto his feet again, scratched his head through his red-flame knit cap, then his nose, then crossed his arms, changed his mind and pushed his hands back into his pockets.

He was broke again. So here he was now, cloaked in shadow directly opposite the Fiesta Bingo Hall, waiting for the chance to take some money off tonight's lucky winner.

A sudden flurry of activity over the road finally drew him from his reverie. The last game of the evening had been played, and it was chucking-out time at last.

The bingo hall's glass doors pushed open and out they came beneath its garish, powder-blue neon sign, tonight's punters, mostly women ranging in age from their twenties to their sixties, and a scattering of fat men who waddled more than walked.

Ronnie ran his deep-set, ill-looking eyes over them as they broke into little groups and strolled up to the bus stop or down to the car park in Milburn Street, laughing and chattering among themselves.

Who'd been lucky tonight, he wondered? That blonde bird in the short skirt looked happy about something, big grin stuck right across her face. Or maybe it was that old bloke with the bald head and the little military moustache? He looked more worried than happy. He was on his own and walking as fast as his arthritic hips would allow. Did that mean he had enough cash in his pockets to be worth robbing?

Ronnie had more or less decided that he had when a sudden eruption of laughter from three old dears who'd just come out of the bingo hall drew his attention.

He shook his head in disgust. Why did they always look so much alike? In their pale blue macs (even though it was the start of summer and there was no chance of rain) and clutching their shopping bags (even though they hadn't been shopping at all), with their white hair teased into perfect waves and curls and their vein-threaded legs sheathed in surgical stockings, they looked so similar they might just as well have been triplets.

Their mood was light. One said something to the other two and flashed her false teeth in a grin, and again they all howled with laughter. Then there was a brief round of arm-patting and earnest *look after yourselves* and two of them started walking up to the bus stop, leaving the third, the old girl with false teeth and thick glasses in transparent blue frames, to head off in the opposite direction alone.

Alone.

Now, thought Ronnie, *she* does *look promising*.

He let the old girl get to the corner of Culshaw Road and Skipton Street, then slid out of the shadows, crossed the road and slouched along oh-so-casually in her wake.

As he had hoped, she turned left into Skipton Street, a narrow thoroughfare full of medium-sized terraced houses, most of which had been converted into offices for solicitors and heating engineers. The curbs on both sides were choked with parked cars. And, like all such side-streets, the lighting was atrocious.

No more than thirty metres ahead, silhouetted against the brighter lights of the shopping precinct at the far end of the street, the old girl was making hard work of getting wherever she wanted to go. Walking seemed to be difficult for her, and she sort of hobbled more than anything else. Ronnie supposed she was in her late sixties or early seventies.

His attention was now focused wholly on her bag. It didn't seem to contain much, but as long as it held a filled purse, he'd be happy.

He glanced back over one sloping shoulder. The shadowy street behind him was empty. He faced front again. Apart from the old girl, it was the same story up ahead. Ronnie began to increase his pace, his trainers making urgent little slaps against the flagstones underfoot.

The old woman kept hobbling along on her stiff joints, humming softly to herself, completely unaware of his presence. As he moved faster, the distance between them decreased, and *still* she didn't know he was there.

His breathing grew rapid now, his heartbeat started to pick up, and he heard the pulses singing in his ears.

A moment later he was close enough to strike.

He lunged forward and grabbed the bag from where it hung over the old woman's right forearm. As he yanked it towards him, the old cow half-turned and cried out, '*Oh my Gawd!*'

Instinctively she held onto the bag, pulling with a strength that surprised him in her determination to retain what was hers.

Ronnie wasn't going to be denied, however. He put everything he had into his next pull and without warning the straps of the shopping bag snapped, so that perpetrator and victim both went stumbling backwards, away from each other.

Ronnie caught his balance. The old woman didn't. With another cry she fell hard and hit her head on one of the flagstones, knocking her glasses loose and sending them skittering into the darkness.

Clutching the bag, Ronnie was suddenly torn between legging it and putting the boot in. Ruled by impulse, he decided to put the boot in, and surging forward, he did just that, kicking his fallen victim, once, twice, a third time.

All the way through it she did nothing but talk, the noisy old bitch. '*Oh my Gawd, no, please, oh Gawd, no . . .* '

Eventually she curled into a ball and Ronnie slackened his assault, leapt over her and took off up Skipton Street in a blur. Even as he ran he delved into the shopping bag, grabbed the old girl's purse and then flung the bag aside.

Thirty metres on, Skipton Street opened out into a brightly-lit pedestrian-only shopping precinct. Without breaking stride, he crossed from one side to the other and then disappeared down another side-street, feeling so good about what had just happened and how smoothly it had all gone that he thought he might actually take to the air at any moment and soar off toward the stars.

He didn't, of course. He just kept running until he reached the end of the street, crossed another road and vanished into the enveloping darkness of Barmy Park.

They called it that because the local library, an ornate red-brick building at the rough centre of the park, had once been an insane asylum. Its real name was Chichester Gardens.

The park gates were locked at sunset, but there was a tree-lined path that led directly from Chichester Road down to the library. Ronnie headed for the library now, his fingers already fumbling the purse open, questing inside. Coins, keys, a bus pass ... he unzipped the side pocket, felt inside.

Yes!

She'd been carrying a fair bit, the crafty old cow!

He snatched out the notes and flung the empty purse into some bushes. Fingering through the wad, he made a quick tally. He reckoned there must be about eighty or ninety quid in all.

At last, breathing hard, he halted in front of Chichester Gardens Library, formally Chichester House Asylum. It was a neat Georgian building two storeys high, with wings branching off to left and right of the central block. Neatly-tended half-moon lawns fronted each of the wings, at the centre of which stood matching displays of conifers, leafy emerald and golden shrubs, and red hawthorns.

Ronnie threw himself down on the steps leading up to the library entrance and caught his breath. He was sweating like a pig, but he was also ninety quid richer.

He was still reflecting on his good fortune when he heard something move in a stand of cherry trees about fifty metres to his left.

Immediately he froze. Maybe he'd disturbed a bird or something. Or maybe it was a couple, indulging in a little kinky sex up against a tree.

He grinned, liking that idea.

But then again, maybe it was someone he'd sooner not meet, someone who fancied preying on *him* the way he'd preyed on the old woman.

He listened some more, but heard nothing. Still . . .

He was an animal and his world was a jungle. Some barely-understood survival instinct told him to seek cover, and he did. He got up quietly, still keeping his eyes fixed on the cherry trees, and stealthily vanished into the bushes in the centre of the half-moon lawn to his right.

Something fluttered overhead, then was gone, and after another quick stab of alarm he allowed himself to relax, for the sound seemed to confirm that he'd disturbed a roosting bird after all.

Anyway, he was busting for a slash. He'd pee, then go buy himself a couple of six-packs at the all-night supermarket. They knew better than to provoke him down there, and had long-since given up trying to challenge him because he was under-age.

He shoved the money into his pocket, un-zipped his fly, spread his legs a little and began to urinate. Again he heard a brief, staccato fluttering overhead, and glanced up.

There was nothing there.

But in that very same moment, something sharp and warm latched onto his exposed manhood and a sudden, fiery burn of agony folded him forward with a sharp cry.

He'd never known pain like it, and

quickly grabbed for the warm, furry *thing* that had bitten into his todger, and wrenched it free. It fought against him, pushing, biting, chattering, and he realized dimly that it had wings, cool, leathery things, that were also working to loosen his grip.

He staggered out of the bushes and threw the creature away from him. It turned end over end and then took to the air, vanishing into the darkness above with a rapid beating of wings.

Before he could examine the damage to his groin, however, he realised that something was moving towards him across the grass, *several* somethings, hopping, walking, flapping and fluttering.

He thought, *Fucking hell! They're bats!*

They leapt up, attached themselves to his legs and started climbing higher. He tried to swipe and kick them loose, but they held tight. He reckoned there were about ten or fifteen of them, and they were *big*, a lot bigger than he'd thought bats could ever be.

More bats were fluttering around his head now, and he tried to swat them away. One tore off his red-flame knit cap. Almost immediately another tangled itself in his long hair. He started mewling, beating himself around the head to keep them at bay, but more bats were throwing themselves at him all the time, deliberately hitting him hard enough to stun and disorientate him —

One fixed itself to the fingers of his left hand and started biting hard. One more smacked him in the right ear. In all the confusion he tripped over his own feet and fell flat on his face.

After that, it was bedlam.

As if by mutual consent, the bats suddenly went for him in what could only be described as a feeding frenzy. His ears filled with their squeaky chattering and excited fluttering. He rolled over, arms and legs lashing out, but the pain of a million bites — or at least what seemed like it — was almost beyond endurance, and served to confuse him even more.

Eventually, overwhelmed by his attackers, his blows began to grow weaker and less effectual with every passing second, until —

Until he caught the sound of footsteps hurrying towards him from the direction of the trees, and he twisted his head as far as he could to see the silhouette of a small man jogging closer.

Oh thank Christ, he thought, *I'm saved* —

He wasn't, though.

The newcomer was carrying a hammer — and the hammer served a very fatal purpose.

5

A little after eight o'clock on Sunday morning, Christopher Deacon was jarred from a deep, dreamless sleep by a persistent ringing at the doorbell.

With an irritable mutter he slowly pushed the warm sheet back off his face and reluctantly set about trying to wake himself up. Beside him, he heard Jan murmur, 'Who . . . ?'

Good question, Deacon thought as he swung his legs out of bed and quickly dry-washed his face. Who would come calling at this hour of the morning?

Stifling a yawn, he dragged himself across the room, took his blue dressing gown from the peg in the back of the door and went downstairs to find out.

Minor, a Jack Russell terrier with a long black and white spotted body and a sleek, all-black head, was standing at the front door, his back legs tensed and his tail wagging furiously as he yapped at the unseen doorbell-ringer. Pushing the dog aside with one naked leg, Deacon unlocked the door and opened it as far as the security chain would allow.

Two men were standing on the path outside the cottage, both wearing suits and ties. Deacon had just enough time to notice that they'd parked a maroon Audi in the gravel lay-by on the other side of the quiet country lane, just behind his own midnight-blue Auris SR, before one of them said, 'Dr Deacon?'

Deacon nodded cautiously. 'Yes?'

The man flashed a warrant card. 'Detective Inspector Sears, sir, Eggerton CID. This is my colleague, Detective Sergeant Ryan. Could we come in for a moment?'

Deacon glanced down at himself. Beneath the open dressing gown he was clad only in creased shorts and a navy blue tee-shirt that read, *I'd Like To Apologise In Advance For My Behaviour Tonight*.

'Well, it's a bit inconvenient,' he croaked.

'Yes, I'm sorry about that,' said Sears,

not sounding sorry at all. 'But murder usually *is*.'

That chased away the last of Deacon's cobwebs, just as it was meant to. His voice dropping a notch, he said, 'Uh, just a moment.'

He closed the door and was slipping the chain free when he heard one of the stairs creak behind him. He turned to find Jan standing about halfway down, wrapped in a peach-coloured dressing gown, watching him through worried eyes.

'It's the police,' he said softly.

Matching his tone she said, 'Yes, I heard. Do you think — ?'

He shook his head. 'I don't know.'

In any case, there was no time now to discuss the matter further. He opened the door and Sears and Ryan came inside. Minor immediately backed away from them, his persistent yap now turning to a throatier growl. Jan hurried down into the hallway and shooed him away.

'Have you found him?' asked Deacon.

Sears treated him to a frown. 'Found whom, sir?' he countered.

Deacon was about to answer, then changed his mind. An awkward silence filled the moment, until Jan came to the rescue with, 'Can I get you some tea or coffee, Inspector?'

Sears looked at her. A little above average height and slim with it, she wore her fine strawberry blonde hair to shoulder-length, with a left-side part. Equally fine eyebrows formed inquisitive arches above her direct pale blue eyes, and there was an appealing pout to her wide mouth that she herself seemed entirely unaware of. Her nose was maybe just slightly too long, he thought, but when she spoke, she revealed excellent teeth.

'Thank you,' he said at last. 'Coffee would be lovely. Milk, no sugar.'

'Sergeant?'

'Coffee'll be fine, thank you.'

That settled, Deacon gestured that they should go through to the lounge. It was a comfortable room with pale lilac walls covered in arty black-and-white prints, and a chunky three-piece suite the colour of coffee beans. Everywhere Sears looked he saw shelves crammed with science- and nature-related books, and pieces of moderately-priced Fenton Art Glass sitting on recessed shelves flanking the chimney breast. A flat-screen TV occupied the wall above the large white fireplace.

When he heard Jan setting out cups in the kitchen, Sears said, 'To answer your question, Doctor, yes — we've found *someone*. Actually, *two* someones. Both dead. Both murdered. Horribly.'

He watched Deacon closely as he said it. Like his wife, Deacon was in his early thirties, of average height and build, and with eyes that were such a deep brown they looked almost black in the early-morning light. With his curly, collar-length blue-black hair and vaguely Mediterranean appearance, he looked more like a male model than a B.Sc.

Thinking to tie his dressing gown at last, Deacon asked uncertainly, 'What has that got to do with me?'

'I'd like to pick your brains,' replied Sears. Without waiting to be asked, he sat down, unclipped the slim, underarm briefcase he'd been carrying and took out a thin stack of ten-by-eights. He set one down on the coffee table. Indelibly stamped with the date and time it had been taken, it showed a section of pale flesh mottled by what appeared to be a series of faintly bruised punctures.

'What are they, do you suppose?' he asked.

Deacon took a pair of retro tortoiseshell glasses from the pocket of his dressing gown and put them on. At last, Sears thought, he looked like a scientist. He studied the image for a moment before saying, 'They appear to be bites, or maybe scratches.'

'They're bites. But what *kind* of bites, Doctor?'

'It's difficult to say, just looking at a photograph.'

'Take a wild guess.'

Deacon hesitated again, then said, 'They're not unlike the kind of punctures a bat might make.'

'That's *exactly* what they are,' said Sears. 'We've even found traces of DSPA in the wounds to confirm it.'

DSPA — *Desmodus rotundus* Salivary

Plasminogen Activator — was a clot-dissolving enzyme secreted by bats to keep their victims' blood flowing while they fed.

Sears continued, 'We found seventy-four separate bites on this body alone, and when the bats had finished with him, the victim was more or less drained of blood. Have you ever come across such a thing before, Doctor?'

Deacon shook his head. 'Never.'

'You sound pretty sure of yourself.'

'I am. In the first place, we don't have any vampire bats here in the United Kingdom. Bats that feed on blood are restricted pretty much to warmer countries — Latin America, the Philippines, Guyana, Suriname, Trinidad and so on. In the second, they're far more likely to attack cattle or other livestock than human beings.'

'And thirdly?'

'Thirdly, at any one feed, the average bat would drink the equivalent of one or two tablespoons of blood, tops. Any more and it would never get off the ground again.'

'So you're saying that bats couldn't have done this?'

'I'm saying I've never heard of it happening before, and that the chances of any bat or colony of bats managing to somehow coordinate an attack on a single victim is so unlikely that it's not even a consideration.'

'What if someone had *taught* them to attack in unison?'

Deacon smiled faintly. 'I'd find that extremely difficult to accept. It's just not possible.' He eyed Sears a little closer. 'Why would you even *consider* such a thing, anyway?'

'Because after the bats had finished with their victims, someone else came along and smashed their brains in.'

'And you think the two are connected in some way?'

'There *has* to be,' said Sears. He fell silent for a moment, then went on, 'Suppose our killer raised these bats from babies. He could train them then, couldn't he?'

'I've never heard of *anyone* being able to train them. I've never heard of anyone even *attempting* to train them. I'm sorry, Inspector, but I simply don't believe it's possible.'

Sears seemed to take that on board. 'How large can bats grow, then?' he asked.

Deacon thought for a moment. '*Petropus vampyrus* is about as big as they get. But they're fruit bats. They're shy, gentle — and *rare*.'

'How big?' prodded Sears.

'They weigh about a kilo, maybe a little more. They can have a wing span of perhaps a metre and a half.'

'That's big,' said Sears. 'But not big enough.'

'I'm sorry?'

Sears threw down a second photo. 'What's the size of your average bat bite?' he asked.

'Three millimetres. Maybe five, at a pinch.'

'This one measured *twelve* millimetres.'

Deacon swept off his glasses. '*What?*'

Just then Jan came back into the room, carrying a tray. Minor trotted along behind her, a green toy bone protruding from his mouth. Ever the gentleman, Ryan hurried to take the tray from her with a polite, 'Thank you, Mrs Deacon.'

'It's *Dr* Deacon, actually,' she corrected him.

'Oh? Like your husband?'

'Yes.'

Minor chose that moment to drop his bone and start growling again.

'Minor . . . ' Jan said warningly.

The dog fell silent.

'That's an unusual name,' remarked Ryan.

Jan said, 'We used to have a Doberman called Major. After he died and we got a smaller dog . . . '

' . . . you decided to call him Minor,' smiled Ryan. 'I like it.'

Clearing his throat to attract Jan's attention, Sears said, 'I know this visit must've caught you on the hop, Dr Deacon. I do appreciate your cooperation.'

'Can I know what this is all about?' asked Jan. She glanced down at the pictures on the coffee table, but Sears quickly turned the top one over.

'I'm afraid not,' he replied. 'Not yet, anyway. I'm sure you understand.'

She looked across at Deacon. His face was unreadable. After another moment she turned and left the room, Minor snatching up his bone and padding out after her.

'Now,' said Sears, getting back to business, 'How do you account for a bat bite that big, Doctor?'

'I don't,' said Deacon.

'You *do* surprise me,' said Sears, picking up his cup and blowing steam off the surface of the coffee. 'I thought you'd have had all the answers, somehow.'

Something in his tone made Deacon bristle. It was as if he had suddenly become a suspect in the investigation. 'What's that supposed to mean?' he asked defensively.

'It's like this, Doctor,' said Sears. 'I need someone who can tell me all about bats, and when DS Ryan here made some enquiries, your name came up. But I'm afraid it came up for the wrong reason.'

'You see, there appears to be a question mark hanging over you. I know you're a highly-respected virologist. I know you were engaged in some highly sensitive work at the Highcroft Research Facility. I know that it involved bats, bats being something a speciality with you, and I know that Highcroft burned to the ground six months ago.'

He took a sip of his coffee. 'I also understand from some of my colleagues that the Government was very quick to step in and stop the police from investigating the matter fully — and I can't help wondering why.'

He fixed Deacon with that flat, penetrating stare of his. 'What *was* it all about, Doctor?' he urged.

Deacon's snort was brief and humourless. 'I only wish I knew myself.'

'*Really?*'

'Really.'

Sears eyed him closely for a long, uncomfortable moment. After what seemed an eternity, he finally said, 'All right, we let it go. For the moment.'

'Does that mean I can go back to bed now?' Deacon asked coldly.

'No, it doesn't,' replied Sears. 'It means

you'd better go shave and put some clothes on, Doctor, because I'd be obliged if you'd come down to the station and review all the evidence — such as it is — first-hand.'

Startled, Deacon stood up quickly. 'What good do you think *I* can do?'

'That remains to be seen,' said Sears. 'But two men have already died, and frankly we need all the help we can get before number three turns up. Besides . . . '

And here he came a step or two closer, and dropped his voice to a low, intimidating hiss. 'I don't know why, but I've got a feeling about this business, Doctor. I've got a feeling that what happened to those two men and whatever happened at Highcroft six months ago are somehow related. And if they *are*, if they died because of some sort of mess you people created, then I should think you'd be grateful for the chance to set things back to rights.'

The silence was heavy and oppressive when he finished. Deacon wanted to hold the other man's stare but couldn't, and hated himself for it. At length he pushed past Sears and headed for the door.

'Where are you going?' snapped Sears.

Deacon paused with his hand on the doorknob. 'To get dressed,' he said tersely.

* * *

It turned out to be a long, trying day, just as Deacon had expected. But by four o'clock that afternoon he felt that he'd done as much as he could, and asked to be taken from the police crime lab, which was located at the nearby University of Eggerton, back to Eggerton Central itself. There, he was shown into Sears' office, invited to take a seat and report his findings.

He put on his glasses, opened the folder he'd been carrying and quickly skimmed through his hand-written notes.

'Well,' he began after clearing his throat, 'as per your instructions, Inspector, I reviewed your case files on the men Terence William Marsh and Ronald Spurgeon, and then, with the assistance of Dr David Schofield, I, ah, examined the bodies.'

He swallowed audibly. That had been

the toughest part of the day for him. He was, after all, a researcher, an academic. His world was the busy laboratory, not the sterile silence of the morgue, and the tools of his trade were test tubes and electron microscopes and bioinformatics databases, not bodies — and especially not bodies which had recently been autopsied and then stitched back together again.

'As unlikely as it seems,' he went on, 'it does appear that both men were attacked by bats and desanguinated. Obviously, I can't comment on the, ah, blows that actually killed them.'

'Next, I went to examine Monk's Tunnel for myself, under the supervision of your Detective Constable Scott. As your scene-of-crime officers had already noted, there's a crude sort of cave — more of a pocket, really — approximately twenty metres into the tunnel that can only be reached by climbing up across the debris that blocks the canal at that point. It measures approximately five metres by eight metres.'

'I investigated this cave by torchlight

and found a number of white, crystalline patches which I took to be dried bat urine. Subsequent analysis of the material at your crime lab confirmed this. I also took various samples of the droppings with which the cave was littered, and analysed them upon my return. I found them to contain, among other substances, nitrogen, phosphorus, ammonia — '

Sears, who had been slouching in his chair, suddenly sat up straight and glanced at Ryan, who was leaning against the closed office door with his arms crossed. 'Ammonia?' he said.

Deacon glanced up. 'Yes. It's what I'd expect to find in bat droppings.'

'That's what we smelled on the dead men, too,' said Sears. 'Go on.'

'Well, although some of the droppings were relatively fresh, the majority were approximately three to four weeks old, which suggests that the cave is no longer being used as a regular roost, but more as a sort of occasional stopping-off point. By their very nature, however, bat droppings are powdery and fragile, so it's difficult to tell their age with absolute certainty. Still, the relative absence of all the things you might reasonably expect to find in the droppings of an indigenous species — mostly insect matter, moth scales, hairs from preening and the like — suggests to me that these were the droppings of *vampire* bats.'

He paused again, glanced over the top of his glasses. Sears nodded for him to go on.

'For the most part, the bites on the bodies measured twelve millimetres, which suggests that you are looking for a member of the megabat family — the Giant golden-crowned flying fox, *Acerodon jubatus*, for example, the large flying fox, *Petropus vampyrus*, or the so-called Spectral bat, *Vampyrum Spectrum*. This, I think, is the most likely of the three, because it is a known carnivore. The others aren't.'

He closed the folder and took off his glasses. 'There is, of course, one other possibility,' he said.

'I'm listening,' said Sears.

'At the moment there are well in excess of a thousand known species of bat in the world,' said Deacon. 'But that's *known* species, Inspector. New ones are coming to light all the time.'

'It could be that we're dealing here with a species that is yet to be identified. I can't imagine how it came to be here, but I think you should bear it in mind.'

'In the meantime, my advice is that you begin a systematic search of every abandoned building, open space and wooded area in Eggerton. If that draws a blank, then I suggest you widen the search to take in any old wells, mineshafts, caves and hollowed-out trees.'

'It's a nice idea,' muttered Sears. 'But a search on that scale costs money and requires more manpower than we can get at the moment. Besides, if these bats *are* being kept as pets or whatever by whoever's finishing off the victims, they won't turn up in any of those places, will they?'

'Well, I'm sorry I can't be more helpful.'

'On the contrary, Doctor, you've been *extremely* helpful.' He sounded almost surprised by the fact.

'Does that mean I can go now?' asked Deacon.

Sears nodded. 'We may need to call on you again, of course, but for now, I'll have a man drive you home immediately.'

Sears was as good as his word, and Deacon got back to the cottage — a picturesque, pink wattle-and-daub structure called *Sombrieul*, after the Sombrieul roses that climbed all over the front elevation — a little after five-thirty. He felt tired and vaguely dejected, and wasn't entirely sure why.

'Was it bad?' asked Jan, as he slumped into an armchair and loosened his tie.

Minor jumped up onto his lap and tried to lick-wash his face by way of greeting. 'Understatement,' he replied, dodging the dog's questing tongue.

'Well, it's all over now,' she said, and squeezed his arm.

She was right, he told himself. But when he went to bed that night, Deacon found sleep impossible. His mind was still racing with thoughts of bats and bodies, of blood and skulls cracked open like breakfast eggs and too many uncomfortable and long-unanswered questions.

He was just getting ready for work at

seven o'clock next morning when the phone in the hallway rang.

'Hello?' he said.

'Hello, Dr Deacon? Its DS Ryan here, sir. Sorry to trouble you again, but Inspector Sears would like you here within the hour.'

Deacon frowned. 'Have you caught him?' he asked eagerly.

'No, sir,' said Ryan. 'But I'm afraid the bugger's struck again.'

6

'Her name was Catherine Weller, and she was twenty-three years old,' said Sears. He was standing at one end of the long, desk-and-chair-strewn office, addressing a team which included DS Ryan, David Schofield, Claire Jarvis, John Richards, three detective constables — one a youngish trainee — and, of course, Deacon himself.

'The story is that she went out with a friend, had a meal, then went on to a club called *Uzi's*, in Beaumont Street. They both got bladdered, and when the friend started becoming abusive, Catherine saw her to the nearest taxi rank, put her in a cab and sent her home. That was approximately ten past midnight.'

'Unfortunately, there weren't any other cabs available at the time, so we're assuming that she decided to make her own way home on foot. Big mistake. A shift worker on his way to work at five-thirty this morning found her stuffed head-first into a wheelie bin on Archer Road.'

'Any CCTV footage that we can check?' asked the Training Detective Constable.

Sears shook his head. 'No. Archer Road's one of the few areas that's not covered yet. But our boy had to get to and from the scene of each crime somehow, so it's worth checking to see if he was picked up on any of the surrounding cameras. Get onto it, Jason.'

The TDC nodded and scribbled something down on the pad in his lap.

'We're sure she's one of ours?' asked one of the detective constables.

Sears glanced over at Schofield for an answer.

'Her head was caved in with the same weapon,' said the pathologist. 'A sixteen-ounce claw-hammer. And of course, she'd received a number of bites, specifically around the trachea, and desanguinated.'

'Any sexual assault?' asked Detective Constable Scott, the officer who'd accompanied Deacon to Monk's Tunnel the day before.

'None,' said Schofield. 'There was only one difference that I could see this time. Everything about the way it happened seems to suggest that she was hammered to death *before* she was bled dry.'

Sears paused a moment to let that sink in. 'Any ideas?' he invited at last.

'Maybe he's finding it harder to control his urges,' suggested Jason, the TDC. 'Can't resist the impulse to hammer them first.'

'Or maybe he's learning as he goes along,' said Deacon, impulsively.

'How's that again, Doc?' asked Sears.

Deacon shifted in his chair, uncomfortably aware that he had suddenly become the centre of attention.

'It could be that he's still new to this thing. Killing, I mean. Maybe he's just realised that it's easier or somehow more convenient to kill his victims before he . . . well, whatever else it is that he does to them.'

'It's possible,' Sears allowed. 'But let's not kid ourselves, Doc. We all *know* what he's doing. He's letting a bunch of trained bats feed off his victims. We just don't know *why* yet.'

'Any theories, Doctor?' asked the other DC.

'None,' said Deacon. 'Most bats are largely shy and gentle by nature. They avoid contact with the outside world whenever possible. They don't go looking for confrontation.'

'And yet our three victims have all been attacked and bled dry by bats,' said Sears. 'That's beyond dispute.'

'I'm not saying it's not happening,' Deacon replied. 'Clearly it *is*. All I'm saying is that you're dealing with something *new* here, something none of us quite understands yet. And because of that, I think you should all tread very carefully and keep an open mind until you know for sure what it is you're up against.'

'But it's not unheard-of for bats to attack humans, is it?' noted Scott.

'No. But they'll only attack humans when they can't take what they need from livestock,' answered Deacon. 'And even then it's not an *attack*, as such, just one small, painless bite. A bat's incisors are so sharp that most victims don't even know they've been bitten at all. In any case, they certainly don't desanguinate their victims. For a bat, that's neither possible nor desirable.'

'It might be, if there's enough of them,' muttered Ryan.

'All right, so we keep an open mind,' said Sears. 'What else have we got? Frank?'

Ryan had been resting his backside against the edge of a desk. Now he pushed himself to his feet. 'I've checked all the zoos and research establishments within a fifty-mile radius,' he said. 'Nobody's reported any escaped bats. I can widen the search, if you like.'

'Do it.'

'I did find out one interesting fact, though,' Ryan continued. 'About two months ago they had some sort of break-in at the Fairway Inner-City Children's Zoo. It's only a small place, exists to give the local kids a chance to pet goats and hamsters, that kind of thing.'

'Go on.'

'Well, whoever broke in killed a goat and a pig, smashed their heads in. At the time, C-Division thought it was just sick-minded vandals getting off on killing a few animals.'

'Don't tell me the animals were bled dry?' said Sears, eyeing him keenly.

'There was blood-loss, certainly, but at the time it was assumed that it had simply soaked into the ground. There was a heavy rain that night, and it washed away a lot of forensics. But now I'm starting to wonder.'

'Were they bitten, these animals?'

'That I can't say. Between you, me and the gatepost, I don't think C-Division was as thorough as they might have been. They just wrote it off to vandals, and the bodies were incinerated shortly afterwards. But if they *were* bitten, it makes you wonder just how long our friend's been around, and why he suddenly graduated from animals to humans.'

Sears turned and studied a map on the wall. 'That Fairway Zoo, whereabouts is it?'

'Lee Road.'

He studied the map for a moment, finally gave the location of the zoo a tap with his finger when he found it. 'So far, then, everything's happened within a three-mile radius of Monk's Tunnel.' He turned back to his team. 'Okay, so what else have we got?'

'I spoke to some of the pest control companies yesterday,' said the second DC. 'About four of them received calls last week from some bloke who wanted bats removed from his property.'

'Whereabouts?'

'That they didn't find out. They just told him that bats are protected by law and to get in touch with English Nature.'

'And did he?'

'English Nature hasn't taken any calls yet.'

'And no-one thought to get the bloke's name or number?'

''Fraid not.'

'Anything else to report?'

The DC said, 'Well . . . '

'Go on.'

'Well, the only other fairly unusual thing I found out was that the rat and pigeon populations of our patch are actually decreasing.'

The TDC grinned. 'Oh well, that's a consolation.'

There was a ripple of grim laughter, across which Deacon cleared his throat.

'Excuse me, Detective Constable,' he said, 'but did they say *why* the rat and pigeon populations had decreased? Has the local authority been making a special effort to eradicate them?'

'No. They've just been receiving less call-outs than usual, and their pest-control officers have noticed a definite drop in numbers.'

'Perhaps they just got tired of city life,' suggested Claire Jarvis, tongue firmly in cheek.

'Or perhaps they've been scared away,' mused Deacon.

Sears glanced at him, his sober expression requesting him to elaborate.

'Well, it's as I said just now,' Deacon went on self-consciously. 'It's quite possible that something new and possibly unprecedented is happening. And if we *are* seeing the emergence of a new species of bat, or a new type of bat behaviour, then maybe the rats and pigeons are aware of it.'

Sears frowned at him. 'I'm not quite

sure what you're suggesting,' he said.

Deacon looked him straight in the face. 'I'm saying that maybe they're getting out of the area while they've still got the chance,' he said quietly.

7

John Cooper slowed his white Ford panel van to a halt and switched off the ignition. He'd parked about halfway along a quiet residential thoroughfare called Saddler Street, just behind a silver-grey Lexus GS. A spare-looking man in a smart grey suit stood beside the car, watching his arrival.

Cooper climbed awkwardly out of the van — awkwardly because he was a tall, broad-shouldered man with a paunch, and once he'd unfolded to his full height he more or less dwarfed the vehicle. 'Mr Metcalf, is it?' he asked as the spare-looking man approached him.

By way of answer the man replied, 'Good morning.' He was about forty, with a lemony, ill-at-ease expression and short, fine black hair that fell loosely across his tanned forehead. Treating his surroundings to a nervous glance, he said, 'Shall we, uh, go inside?'

Cooper turned and studied the property outside which they had both parked. It was a tall, narrow, red brick house, Victorian in design, with wide bay windows and a portico entrance. All the houses in Saddler Street were identical. What they lacked in width, they made up for in length and height.

Cooper was a few years older than his companion, with a square, ruddy face, an affable manner and a dusting of neatly-barbered red-fair hair. He wore a pair of creased coveralls, at the open neck of which could just be seen a blue tee-shirt.

'I'll have a look around outside first, if that's all right,' he said, and when Metcalf nodded, he went to the back of the van, upon the panels of which had been painted J COOPER LTD PEST CONTROL EST 1995. He unlocked the doors and rummaged through a confusion of pesticides, rat traps, insect sprays and sticky boards until he'd gathered together an aluminium stepladder, a flashlight and a pair of heavy-duty gauntlets.

As he was locking up again, an elderly man came to the door of the house next door and called out, 'Hello, Mr Metcalf. You come to do somet'in' about them bats at last?'

Metcalf turned to the newcomer and said patiently, 'Hello, Mr Okonkwo. Yes, we're going in to have a look around now.'

As he held onto the doorframe for support, the old man studied Cooper through curious eyes. 'Tha's a good t'ing,' he said. 'I don' like livin' next door to no bats.'

'Well, you won't have to put up with them for much longer,' said Metcalf. He turned back to Cooper. 'Right. Shall we make a start?'

With a nod, Cooper followed him up the black and white tiled path to the front door.

Metcalf had called him late on Friday afternoon. He'd said he had a house he was planning to renovate, but that when he'd gone in to have a look around and see what needed to be done, he'd heard some sort of commotion up in the loft, a kind of panicky, fluttering sound.

Cooper had immediately said, 'Pigeons, eh?'

'No, I don't think so,' Metcalf had replied. 'The old gentleman next door says he's seen them flying in and out at dusk. He seems to think they're bats.'

Cooper had smiled at that. 'He could be right,' he allowed. 'But if they *are* bats, there's not a lot I can do about it. They're protected, see.'

'Protected?' repeated Metcalf.

'Wildlife and Countryside Act 1981,' Cooper explained. 'That and the Natural Habitats Regulations of 1994 make it a criminal offence to disturb or otherwise remove 'em. Especially at the moment.'

'Oh? Why's that?'

'Between May and August they give birth to their young. Certainly can't touch 'em then.'

'Oh,' Metcalf said again.

He sounded disappointed, but Cooper got the feeling he wasn't telling the property developer anything he didn't already know. It was safe to assume that Metcalf had called all the major companies before calling him. Maybe he was hoping that Cooper didn't know the rules and regulations, that he might just get rid of them anyway because he didn't know any different.

'Is there nothing I can do?' asked Metcalf, clearly fishing now. 'I really need to get my men in there and put the place on the market as soon as possible.'

Cooper considered telling him to have a word with a local wildlife group. They could send someone around to assess the situation and maybe suggest ways he could go ahead with his renovations without causing the bats undue distress. But he sensed an opportunity here to make a few quid on the side.

'Costing you money, is it?' he asked.

'Well, obviously I want to get the place renovated and back on the market as soon as possible,' Metcalf confessed.

'I suppose I could come and have a look, see what I could do to help you out,' he suggested. 'Of course, we'd have to keep it strictly between the two of us.'

It was exactly what Metcalf had been hoping he'd say. 'Naturally,' he said keenly. 'What, ah, kind of money are we talking about?'

Money. The word was music to Cooper's

ears. He'd recently gone through a very messy divorce and his maintenance payments to Anne for the two boys were bleeding him dry. It would be nice to have a few extra quid to play with for a change.

'I'll have to take a look before I can tell you that,' he'd said. 'But from the sounds of it, we're talking at least five hundred.'

Metcalf thought about that, then said, 'When do you want to have a look?'

'Monday morning, all right?'

'I'll meet you there. Say about nine-thirty?'

'Nine-thirty it is.'

And now here they were, Cooper following Metcalf through the front door and into a bright hallway with a high, textured ceiling, their feet clattering on the bare boards underfoot.

As Cooper temporarily stowed his gear behind the front door, Metcalf said, 'Once we get rid of the bats, my chaps can really get to work. I'm going to put down bleached oak boards, install a marble mantelpiece in the living room with a limestone hearth . . . '

Only half-listening, Cooper followed

Metcalf along the hallway, past the doors to two reception rooms and on into a kitchen with a skylight through which Monday morning sunshine fell in a white cascade. The entire place had been gutted. There were no cupboards, no furniture, nothing, and the walls had been stripped back to the original, dark plaster. 'Big job, when you finally get around to it,' he noted.

Metcalf unlocked the back door and led him out into a long, overgrown garden that backed onto a high wall of graffiti-stained corrugated iron.

'Don't think much of the view,' Cooper commented.

Metcalf shook his head. 'No. But this is an up and coming area. It's being developed left, right and centre.'

While Metcalf was talking, Cooper examined a long, narrow window at ground level which had been broken and boarded up with what appeared to be a rain-stained sheet of plywood. 'See, this is your trouble,' he said, cutting the other man off. 'You need to proof your place properly, or you'll get all sorts in. What's behind there, anyway?'

'The cellar.'

'Well, it's probably running alive with rodents now,' Cooper stated, more to scare the other man than out of any real conviction that mice had moved in.

He walked backwards and forwards along the back of the house, studying the window sills and the junctions between the wall and the ground. He bent and studied an accumulation of long, dark brown droppings, each no more than a centimetre in length. They crumbled between Cooper's thumb and forefinger when he squeezed them.

With a theatrical sigh, he walked down to the bottom of the long, narrow garden, where he shielded his blue eyes from the sunlight and looked back up at the house. It wasn't unheard of for bats to roost in gable ends, behind barge boards or cavity walls. But when Cooper spotted the two slipped slates beside the chimney breast, he saw clearly where Metcalf's bats had been getting in and out.

He knew then that this job was going to be money for old rope. All he had to do was force the bats to leave and then proof the hole to stop them coming back. After that, Metcalf could get one of his own blokes in to replace the slipped tiles and hey presto, job done. But he wasn't about to let the property developer know that.

He waded back through the tall grass, shaking his head regretfully. 'You've definitely got a bat infestation,' he announced when he was close enough. 'A big one, if the accumulation of droppings is anything to go by. But I reckon I can do something for you.'

'For five hundred,' Metcalf said quickly.

For a moment Cooper was tempted to go higher, say six-fifty. But he didn't want to be greedy and lose the job altogether. 'Five hundred, yeah,' he replied. 'Cash, of course. Do you want to go ahead with it?'

Metcalf said worriedly, 'There's not going to be any comeback, is there? From the police or anything?'

'Not if we both keep *shtum*,' said Cooper.

Metcalf nodded. 'All right.'

'Lovely job. Just let me go up and take a look in your loft.'

They went back inside, Metcalf locked

the back door and they clattered through the house, footsteps echoing hollowly on the worn, bare boards.

Neither man noticed the green cellar door to their left open a crack as they passed by.

★   ★   ★

'Blimey, you'll have to be fit to live here,' Cooper remarked. He'd never been big on exercise. He'd always drunk and smoked far more than was good for him, and consequently he was breathing hard by the time they reached the second floor. Still, there was only one more flight of stairs to go and then they would reach the bathroom, in the ceiling of which Metcalf had told him they would find the loft hatch.

By this time, Metcalf was too preoccupied to reply. Nervy by nature, he was keenly aware that what he had just engaged Cooper to do was illegal. All the other pest companies he'd called had left him in no doubt about that. But what else was he to do?

At last they reached a narrow landing at the top of the house and Metcalf opened a door that led into an oblong-shaped room. As with the rest of the house, it had been gutted. But Metcalf was clearly a man with a vision. 'I'm going to fit a twelve-jet whirlpool bath just here,' he said, some of his earlier enthusiasm returning. 'A Victorian basin over there, a high-level WC with a rosewood toilet seat . . .'

Only half listening, Cooper went over to the single large sash window set in the right-side wall. It looked out onto a row of long, narrow gardens, beyond which stood the cleared patch of ground that lay behind the graffiti-smeared iron sheeting he'd seen from downstairs.

'It's up there, I take it,' he said, interrupting Metcalf's sales pitch.

Metcalf glanced up at the hatch overhead and said, 'Oh, yes.'

They listened for a moment, but could hear nothing. With a shrug, Cooper set out his stepladder and put one heavy-booted foot on the first rung.

That was when they heard an odd

creak-cum-dragging sound from some-where downstairs.

Metcalf almost leapt out of his shoes. He breathed, 'What the devil was that?'

'Search me,' Cooper said helpfully.

Metcalf hesitated for another moment. Then, because it gave him an excuse to leave the room before the loft hatch was shoved back and Cooper went up there to deal with the bats that had been causing him so much inconvenience, he said, 'I'd better go and take a look. I'll, ah, leave you to it . . .'

In the next moment he was gone.

Cooper shook his head, pulled on his gauntlets and checked to make sure his flashlight was working okay. Once again he began to climb the ladder, but once again he was interrupted by a sound from somewhere below.

This time it sounded like a cry, and it was followed by an unmistakable thud.

Cooper frowned now. He wondered if Metcalf had been joined by a colleague of some sort, or whether the silly sod had slipped and hurt himself. Either way, he felt it might be better to go and find out before he went up into the loft. After all, he didn't want to get caught mucking around with a protected species if he could help it.

Setting the flashlight down on the top step of the ladder, he went back out onto the landing and peered over the banister. All he could see from this angle was the deep stairwell flanked by the other banister rails, corkscrewing their way down to the ground floor. He listened but heard nothing, and after a moment called, 'You all right down there Mr Metcalf?'

There was no reply, and he felt a stir of irritation. If Metcalf had chickened out on him at the last moment . . .

But then there was that dragging, creaking sound, the cry and the thud.

'Mr Metcalf?'

Silence.

He wondered now if Metcalf had surprised someone who shouldn't have been down there, a squatter or something, and come a cropper.

'Hello?' he called.

He went to the head of the stairs,

pulling off his gauntlets as he did so. After a moment's hesitation, he began to descend.

'You all right, mate?' he said, more because he wanted to replace the ominous silence with sound and let whoever was down there know he was coming so they'd have plenty of time to scarper.

He went down to the second floor, along the landing, to the head of the second flight of stairs. Around him, the empty house hissed with silence.

It was only when he reached the head of the second flight of stairs that he finally saw Metcalf and the thing that had killed him.

* * *

Because it was the last thing he'd been expecting to see, he didn't even realize it was Metcalf at first. All he saw was a suit-clad body sprawled on its back halfway down the stairs, its arms and legs akimbo, the left side of its head smashed in, and claret-coloured blood soaking into the dry boards beneath it.

Then he saw the thing crouching over the body.

It looked like a man, and yet it wasn't like any man that Cooper had ever seen before. Its head snapped up as he appeared at the top of the stairs and its dark, down-turned lips peeled back to reveal sharp white teeth in an angry hiss. A second later it straightened to its full height — maybe five feet seven or eight.

The man-thing was holding a hammer in its right claw. The head of it was stained red, and furred-up with bits of Metcalf's hair.

As the thing stepped over Metcalf and began to ascend the stairs, its head sunk low into its narrow shoulders and something glutinous dripped off the weapon to leave a jellified red trail in its wake.

Cooper's faced drained of colour. He stood frozen for valuable seconds as his mind struggled to grasp what his eyes were telling him. Then he snapped back to reality and yelled something — a swear word, he thought — and threw his gauntlets at the creature, as if they might actually slow or stop its otherwise fluid ascent.

They didn't, of course, and Cooper turned and ran, grabbing the banister rail and dragging himself along to make better speed, up the third flight onto the narrow landing, into the bathroom-to-be.

He slammed the door behind him, reached for the bolt and swore again because the place had been gutted and there *was* no bolt. Pulses hammering, he glanced around. There was nothing with which to brace the door. He could use the stepladder, but if that didn't hold he was in real trouble.

He crossed to the window, his breath a raspy wheeze now, but he already knew there'd be no escape that way.

His only chance lay in the loft. It was just possible that he could hold off whoever or whatever had killed Metcalf from up there.

Without wasting further time, he grabbed his flashlight, shinned up the stepladder, forced back the loft hatch and used his elbows to lever himself up into the darkness beyond.

For a heart-stopping moment he didn't think he was going to make it, that he was going to fall backwards and land flat on his arse when that thing finally smashed through the door and came to get him. But then he made one last, desperate effort and all at once he was there, scrambling into the loft, sprawling flat on his ample belly, then rising to his hands and knees, grabbing the hatch and slamming it back into place.

He was in almost complete darkness now, his only company his own ragged breathing.

With shaking hands he searched his pockets for his mobile phone. Where . . . ? Sod it! He'd left it in the van! Never mind. You're safe up here. He can't get you here. *It* can't get you.

His eyes began to adjust to the gloom. What was that thing, anyway? Again he saw its face in his mind, and shuddered. It was so close to a face, and yet it wasn't. Everything about it had seemed . . . distorted, somehow, as if the face itself had been fashioned from wax and the wax had been heated ever-so-gently to make the features ooze just a *little* out of place.

Then all thought stopped dead.

He heard a sound down below.

The thing had just opened the bathroom door.

Straining, he could just about hear the soft slide-and-creak it made on the bare floorboards.

John Cooper was hardly breathing at all now. He hunched over the hatch, ready to hold it down with his considerable body-weight should the thing that had killed Metcalf try to come up and kill him, too.

He heard the thing circling the step-ladder below, imagined its dark, wide-apart eyes studying the bathroom ceiling, the hatch.

And then —

He heard a voice.

It was so soft that he almost didn't hear it at all. But then he caught the soft sibilant hiss of the words, and a graveyard tingle washed through him.

'*Ele tem de morrer, meninos pequenos.*'

Silence again.

Cooper wondered if the thing was talking to itself or trying to communicate with him. His teeth clenched. His brother-in-law had made some pretty nasty threats against him after he split up with Anne, and he'd taken to carrying a long block of wood he called Suzy Q in the van. If he had Suzy here now . . .

But he didn't.

He had sod all.

'*Nós não podemos mostrar a mercé, só esta vez?*' hissed the voice.

Cooper could hear it clearer now, and realised with a start that the thing had climbed the ladder and put what passed for its face against the other side of the hatch. He leapt back from it as if burnt.

Then he heard a soft chittering sound somewhere behind him, and finally understood that the thing downstairs hadn't been talking to him at all, but rather to the bats he'd been coming up here to evict.

His head snapped around. Light fell into the loft from the hole he'd spotted earlier, by the chimney breast. Sunshine puddled on old rafters and dirty fibreglass insulation. He thought he saw something move just beyond the light, but most of the loft was still as black as tar and he couldn't be sure.

The clicking, squeaking sounds came again, and this time he snatched up the flashlight, aimed it at the noise and switched it on.

Oh Christ.

A beam of dusty yellow light knifed across the loft, and he had just time enough to see what appeared to be a brown velvet curtain hanging from the roof supports, and to think, stupidly, *A brown velvet curtain?*, before the curtain that wasn't a curtain at all burst apart in a flurry of angry movement, and all at once bats were everywhere, bats larger than he'd ever seen before, squeaking, fluttering, twisting and swooping.

Cooper screamed and dropped the flashlight. Its beam rippled across the loft, giving him a brief glimpse of the bats as they came at him, the sound of their flapping wings a furious, deafening sound in the confined space. One threw itself at the hands he'd crossed protectively over his face. He cried out and swayed. Another smacked him in the back of the head, and he quickly shifted one hand to protect his balding pate.

The bats came at him from all directions, slapping into him with the full weight of their heavy, furry bodies, making sure that he was kept constantly off-balance and given no chance to gather his wits.

His mind now little more than a confusion of half-formed thoughts, he lurched awkwardly to his feet, thinking that perhaps if he made it as far as the hole in the roof he could shove his head outside and scream for help.

With bats crashing into him, clawing at his hair, scratching his hands, he took one struggling step, then another, then —

Then his foot missed one of the rafters and plunged right through the plasterboard of the bathroom ceiling.

He went down hard, smashing his groin against the rafter he'd just missed. He screamed, tried to pull his trapped leg free, but the bats were all around his head now, trying to nip and bite him.

At last he dragged himself back to his feet, but by this time he was so disorientated that he took three steps before he realised that he was going the wrong way. He turned, still trying to swat the fluttering bats away from his half-closed eyes, took another step and stumbled over the fallen flashlight. He slammed hard against the rafters, his face sinking deep into a section of dusty insulation.

They were on him then, coming to rest quickly on his head and neck and shoulders, biting, gouging, tearing at every inch of his exposed flesh, and the sounds they made as their blood-lust reached its height were almost enough to burst his eardrums.

Cooper's feet kicked a desperate tattoo. He tried to push himself up but the weight of ten, twenty, thirty, forty bats, a writhing, chattering, fluttering, feeding mass of them, held him down, kept his face buried deep into the fibreglass insulation. He wanted to scream, but couldn't even find enough air to breathe.

The bats continued to bite and scratch and crawl over their victim, covering him in a writhing, heaving, chittering shroud. And after a while John Cooper's struggles died to nothing, and he lay deathly still.

8

As soon as the briefing ended, Deacon caught Sears' eye and asked a trifle impatiently, 'Can I go now, Inspector?'

Sears didn't even have to think about his answer. 'I'd prefer it if you stuck around for a while, if you don't mind.'

'But I have a job to go to.'

'Don't worry about that. I'll square things away with your boss.'

'It's not that I'm concerned about. I just don't see what further use I can be to you *here*.'

'Well, for a start, you could step across to the lab and review the forensics on the Weller case for me,' said Sears.

Realising then that there was little point in arguing about it, Deacon bit off whatever response he'd intended to make. For reasons of his own — and Deacon had a shrewd idea what they might be — Sears wanted to keep him within easy reach. So he snatched up his briefcase and made his way down to the University of Eggerton, and was reviewing the bat-related forensics — such as they were — at the crime lab a couple of hours later when one of the technicians took a phone call.

'Dr Deacon?' the girl said after she rang off.

'Yes?'

'DI Sears would like to see you ASAP.'

Deacon gathered his notes together and walked back to Eggerton Central. Sears, surveying his department thoughtfully from the comfort of his small, glass-walled office, gestured for him to come in, close the door behind him and take a seat. As he did so, Sears flipped a Home Office fax across the desk.

'Read it,' he said.

Deacon put his glasses on and quickly scanned the page. It was a temporary release from both the Official Secrets Act and the confidentiality clause in his contract with the Highcroft Research Facility.

A cynical smile quirked briefly at his mouth. As he'd suspected, this was what

Sears had been waiting for, the reason he'd wanted to keep him around.

'All right,' he said softly. 'What do you want to know?'

Sears said, 'Everything. To begin with, what exactly were you doing at Highcroft?'

Deacon shrugged. 'You're in the front line, Inspector. You must know that infectious diseases are emerging and re-emerging all the time. There are more than fifteen hundred different types of bacteria, virus, parasite and fungi out there, and they all have the potential to wipe us out quicker than thought. We do what we can to protect ourselves, but these things are mutating all the time, developing resistance to traditional medicines — that's when drugs can make a difference to *begin* with.

'Well, about a year ago I was engaged to assist Professor Victor Santoro in researching treatments to combat the Ebola and Marburg viruses, both of which are carried by bats, but to which the bats themselves are immune. Essentially, our task was to isolate the antibodies in the bats' blood and develop

114

them into vaccines to combat these filoviruses.'

'So you were experimenting with bats?' Sears prodded.

'We used bats in our research,' Deacon corrected him.

'How many?'

'Fifty. All males.'

'And where did they come from?'

'We used a reputable supplier — '

'I don't mean that. I mean where did they come from *originally*?'

'Is that relevant?'

'I don't know. But I'd sooner know than *not* know.'

'All right. They came from Brazil. They're a species known there as *Grande agressivo morcego*.'

'Which means . . . ?'

'Literally, large, aggressive bat.'

'How large were they?'

Deacon made a few quick mental calculations. 'Not as large as the largest, but a fair size. From tip to tail, about half a metre. They weighed about a kilogram, and had a wing span of little more than a metre.'

Sears grimaced. 'And *are* they any more aggressive than other bats?'

'Yes. But most bats are — '

' — shy and gentle, yes, I remember.'

'The Brazilians we were using had more . . . 'attitude', I suppose you could call it. But they weren't violent unless provoked.'

'Why did you use them at all? They must have been pretty dangerous to work with.'

'They were. They *are*. But of all the species, *Grande agressivo morcego* enjoys the closest relationship to man. That made it idea for our purpose.'

Sears sighed. 'All right. Go on.'

'Well, there really isn't much more to tell. Research went the way research always goes, slowly, methodically, a process of trial-and-error.'

'Until Highcroft burned down.'

'Yes.'

'What did you make of the fire, Doc?'

'I still think it was the work of animal rights extremists,' said Deacon. 'The thinking at the time was that it was down to a group known as UnEthical. Of all the animal rights activists, they were known to be the most militant.'

'So you reckon they got in, rescued all the bats and then fire-bombed the place?'

'More or less.'

'It sounds reasonable. But it doesn't quite hold water, does it?'

'Doesn't it?' countered Deacon.

'I've seen the files,' said Sears. 'What files the Government will trust me with, at any rate. Fire investigators found no signs of forced entry, and no tracks in the immediate vicinity that they couldn't account for. They gave all known members of UnEthical a tug, and without exception each one could account for his or her movements at the time of the fire. And it doesn't explain what happened to your boss, does it? Professor Santoro disappeared on the night of the fire, and no one knows what became of him.'

Deacon pinched the skin between his eyebrows. 'I always felt that he surprised whoever was trying to burn the place down. I think he might have been killed trying to stop them, and his body taken away, or maybe kidnapped by them.'

'It was Santoro you were asking about yesterday morning, wasn't it?' said Sears. 'When you'd asked if we'd found him yet.'

Deacon said reluctantly, 'Yes.'

'Tell me about Santoro, Doc. What kind of man was he?'

As he drew breath, Deacon noticed a photograph on one of the shelves behind Sears. It was a studio portrait of a smiling brunette with a dark-haired girl of about seven sitting on her lap, presumably Sears' wife and daughter. They both looked very happy.

'He was a brilliant, dedicated scientist,' he said at last. 'We enjoyed a good working relationship, and got along well on a social level.'

'Did he have any family?'

'Back home in Brazil, yes. He came from quite a prominent family, I believe, but he never spoke much about them.'

'Brazil?' repeated Sears.

'Yes. He was Brazilian.'

'Like the bats?'

Deacon snorted. 'And what's that supposed to mean?'

118

For the first time since Deacon had known him, a tired smile relaxed some of the muscles in Sears' stern face. 'Christ knows,' he replied honestly. 'Just a coincidence, I suppose.'

'Not really. Santoro had studied *Grande agressivo morcego* for years before he came to work in Britain. It was a species he understood and knew how to handle.'

'His 'bat of choice', you might say,' suggested Sears.

'That's one way of putting it, certainly.'

'What did Santoro seem like in the run-up to his disappearance? He must have been under pressure to get results.'

'We're all under pressure, Inspector. I don't think Victor was under any more than the next man.'

'Could he have had personal problems, though? A tangled love life?'

'I really couldn't say.'

'Well, was there anyone else in his life at all? A woman? A *man*?'

'Not that I know of.'

'So everything was perfectly normal right up until the moment he vanished.'

'Yes.'

But it wasn't. The strain of working long hours, often seven days a week, had begun to take its toll on Santoro. He had grown more preoccupied than usual, and Deacon had found himself catching and correcting more and more silly mistakes in his notes. But even now, six months on, friendship and loyalty made him reluctant to speak ill of the methodical, softly-spoken Brazilian.

'How did he feel about experimenting on animals?' Sears continued.

'We never really discussed it, but the same as me, I should think. It's a necessary evil. We do it for the good of mankind, but that doesn't mean we have to enjoy it. In any case, we weren't experimenting on the bats. All we were doing was taking samples of their blood for analysis.'

Suddenly restless, he sat forward. 'Is it really necessary to rake this up all over again, Inspector? I answered all these questions six months ago. It's ancient history now.'

'Not for *you*,' said Sears. 'I can see it in your eyes, Doc. You want to know what happened to Santoro.'

'Of course I do. You don't work closely with someone for six months without developing some kind of feeling for them. I had the highest regard for Victor, both as a scientist and a human being, and I believe the feeling was mutual. *Something* happened the night of the fire, but what? It would be nice to find out.'

'Yes. About Santoro *and* those bats.'

Deacon shook his head. 'There you go again. You're looking for some kind of link where there isn't one.'

'You don't *know* that. We've got bats attacking human beings. You had fifty particularly aggressive ones that went missing.'

'Yes. But you're overlooking something. Our bats came from the Brazilian rainforest. They were used to temperatures of thirty-five degrees Celsius, both there and in our laboratory. How long do you think they'd have lasted in the British countryside, just as autumn was turning to winter?'

'You believe they're all dead by now?'

'Yes.'

'Then why did the Government step in so quickly to shut the police investigation down? What did they have to hide?'

'Nothing. But we had a General Election last November. It was a very sensitive time for a government that's been accused of more incompetence than . . . than you've made arrests. Avian flu, hoof-and-mouth . . . They wanted to make sure that what happened at Highcroft didn't give the Opposition any extra ammunition.'

He paused. 'In any case, the Government's experts were of the same opinion as me. There was no way *Grande agressivo morcego* could survive a British winter.'

'Unless someone took them in and kept them warm right through till spring,' Sears replied grimly.

Before Deacon could form a response, there was a brisk rapping at the glass door and Ryan poked his head in. 'Sorry to interrupt,' he said crisply. 'But our bloke's struck again.'

Sears swore, came up out of his chair and grabbed his jacket. 'Whereabouts?'

'Saddler Street,' said Ryan. 'And from the sound of it, the bugger's done *two* this time.'

9

On the way to Saddler Street, Ryan told them as much as he knew.

'Apparently someone turned up there this morning to get rid of some bats. About half-an-hour later the old man next door heard a commotion, panicked, and called the police. C-Division sent an area car to take a look, and they found two bodies.'

'Bitten, like the others?'

'No to the first one, yes to the second.'

'And the bats?'

'Gone.'

Sears sucked at one cheek. 'Have we identified the bodies yet?'

'Small-time property developer name of Metcalf, self-employed pest controller named Cooper.'

They reached Saddler Street ten minutes later. The immediate vicinity had been cordoned off to the gathering crowd, and a number of police Astras,

BMWs and Mercedes Incident Support Unit Sprinters were parked everywhere. As he climbed out of Sears' Audi, Deacon even spotted a dog unit van nearby.

He felt as apprehensive now as he had when the news had first come in. In fact, he'd been growing increasingly apprehensive ever since Sears had first barged into his life twenty-four hours earlier.

Not that he could really blame Sears for that. No: what was bothering Deacon was the growing possibility that there really *could* be a connection between the events at Highcroft and the recent murders.

At first he hadn't believed it possible. Or maybe he simply hadn't *wanted* to believe that it was possible. But Sears had made a very good point earlier on. Coincidence could only stretch so far.

As soon as he got out of the car, Sears was greeted by the Senior Investigating Officer, a tall, slim woman with short brown hair, who introduced herself as Detective Inspector Liz Hicks. After Sears introduced his companions, she brought them up to speed in a few brief sentences.

'Christ alone knows what happened here,' she began. 'But the way I read it is this: these two men, Metcalf and Cooper, came in to take a look at Metcalf's bat problem. According to the old man next door, bats had been roosting in the loft for at least the last three weeks. Anyway, they came in, went upstairs and disturbed whoever was already in residence.'

'The bats, you mean?'

'Bats — and a third man.'

Sears exchanged a glance with Ryan. 'Go on.'

'Looks as if he'd been living in the cellar for a while. We found faeces, a crude sort of bed made up of rags . . . and an awful lot of bones.'

'*Bones?*' echoed Ryan.

DI Hicks nodded. 'Mostly mice, as near as I can tell. Looks to me as if he'd been eating them.'

'Jesus.'

'My sentiments exactly,' agreed the SIO. 'David Schofield's just arrived. He's had a quick look at the bodies, and just started working on the first one now. Everything's still in situ.'

'Thanks, Liz.'

'Well, I'd heard you were after some PQMS in connection with a series of bat attacks. That's why I gave you a shout straight away.'

'I appreciate it,' replied Sears. Turning to Deacon, he said confidentially, 'This isn't going to be very pleasant, Doc. If you'd sooner wait out here — '

Nothing would have given Deacon greater pleasure, but he forced himself to say, 'No, no, I'll be okay.'

With more than a little trepidation he followed Sears, Ryan and DI Hicks up the tiled front path and helped himself to a pair of disposable gloves. To distract himself as he slipped them on, he caught Ryan's eye and asked quietly, 'PQMS?'

Ryan mouthed, 'Person of Questionable Mental Stability.'

'Ah.'

The house was a confusion of activity. Scene of crime officers were looking for clues and painstakingly cataloguing whatever they found. The place was being systematically photographed from every angle, and a fingerprint man who had just finished dusting the ground-floor banister rail was now using low-tack tape to transfer the results to an acetate sheet.

They followed DI Hicks through the house and into the gutted kitchen. She was a plain-faced, authoritative woman in her middle thirties, her movements quick and businesslike.

Set into the right-side wall, just behind the kitchen door, was another wider, lower door constructed from four-inch planks that had been painted a sickly green. This door had been pulled open to reveal a narrow, wooden staircase, which descended to the cellar below.

'Better cover your noses,' Hicks advised. 'It stinks to high heaven down there.'

She led the way down into a cramped, mean-looking room lit by a single low-watt electric bulb, and she was right — it stunk eye-wateringly of human waste. The cement between its bare red-brick walls was crumbling, and the junction between wall and ceiling was festooned with thick, dirt-encrusted spider webs. The cracked concrete floor, once painted with red tile paint that was now flaking, was littered with piles of human excrement and a puddle or two of urine. From the look of the well-used bench and empty shelves, some previous owner had converted it into a workshop. Now, if the soiled rags draped over it were anything to go by, the bench doubled as a bed.

A number of tiny, gnawed bones littered the floor around the bench. Bluebottles were busily exploring those few carcasses that still had meat or fur clinging to them. A couple of Little Nipper mousetraps in one corner still held putrefying bodies.

From the corner of his eye, Sears saw Deacon sway a little and snapped, 'Get him out of here, Frank.'

Deacon, feeling more sick than foolish, allowed the DS to hustle him upstairs again. A few moments later Sears and DI Hicks joined them in the kitchen. Deacon still looked pale and sweaty, his brown-to-black eyes watery.

'Want to get some fresh air?' asked Sears.

'No. I'm okay.'

'I wish *I* was,' Sears muttered fervently.

They found David Schofield examining Neil Metcalf's body on the second floor stairway. John Richards, the Senior SOCO, was assisting him. Sight of the dead man, the side of his head smashed in, turned Deacon's queasy stomach still more, but he swallowed hard and tried to remain professionally detached.

Sears nodded a terse greeting. 'What have we got, Dave?'

'Two hammer-blows to the left side of the head. I don't suppose he knew much about the second one.'

'But no bites?'

'None.'

'Where's the other body?'

'In the loft. I haven't had the chance to make anything more than a preliminary visual examination yet.'

'All right,' said Sears, glancing at his companions. 'Let's go up and take a look for ourselves.'

Again DI Hicks led the way, up past Schofield, Richards and the body, along the second floor landing and up the third flight of stairs to the top floor, where the woman paused to hand out flashlights.

Then they followed her into a small room with a large sash window set in the right-side wall.

An aluminium ladder in the middle of the bare floor disappeared into the darkness beyond the opened loft hatch. To one side of it, a ragged hole had been punched down through the ceiling. John Cooper's stepladder, which had already been checked for forensics, was leaning against the opposite wall.

Hicks stood aside and Sears took the lead, climbing carefully, followed by Ryan, then Deacon.

Scene-of-crime officers had already set up arc lamps, but wouldn't switch them on until Schofield had completed his initial examination of the body in case the heat they threw out contaminated or otherwise distorted his findings. When they were all safely balanced on the rafters, Sears shone his flashlight on the dead man, who lay flat on his stomach about six metres away. All three covered their mouths and noses again because of the sour, ammonia-like stench that filled the loft.

'They've had a field day here,' Ryan murmured, picking his way over to the body and being careful not to hit his head on the roof supports.

Deacon, his professional curiosity finally getting the better of him, began to examine the rest of the loft, playing his flashlight into every nook and cranny. Some of the supports held tiny, deep scratches or gouges where the bats had hung upside down during the hours of daylight. The rafters and insulation immediately below them was thick with accumulated droppings.

'What can you tell us, Doc?' asked Sears. For once, his voice was curiously hushed.

Deacon said, 'Well, there was a colony up here, that's for sure, perhaps thirty or forty-strong. And they've been here for some time, if the droppings are any indication, maybe even longer than the three weeks the old man next door reported. They got in and out through that hole over there, beside the chimney breast.' His eyes fell to the body and he added, 'That poor devil didn't stand a chance, trapped in here with them.'

The dead man's neck, ears and hands

were all covered in bites. He could only imagine Cooper's utter terror as the bats had overwhelmed him and he realised that there wasn't a single thing he could do to stop —

Suddenly he frowned, dropped to his knees beside the body and shone the flashlight slowly along its left side. Sears and Ryan swapped a look. Then Sears said, 'What is it?'

After a moment, Deacon said, 'I need a set of tongs or forceps.'

'What?'

'Here, look! Can you see?'

He trained the flashlight on a barely-visible triangle of shiny, membranous iron-grey skin that was protruding from beneath the body. Frowning, Sears said, 'What is it?'

'I believe it's the tip of a bat's wing,' Deacon said shakily, and now his voice was hushed, too. 'The dead man may have smothered it when he fell.'

Sears told Ryan, 'Get David up here with some forceps or tongs, quick as you can.'

Ryan hurried back to the loft hatch and

called down his request. A few moments later, the overweight pathologist wheezed up the ladder and through the hatch. 'What is it?' he asked, carefully getting to his feet and coming closer with a set of forceps in his right hand.

'Deacon's found one of the bats, but we'll have to move the body before we can retrieve it.'

It was vital that Schofield supervise any such action, to prevent any mishandling that might leave deceptive marks on the corpse. 'Is it still alive?' he asked, crouching on the other side of the dead man.

'I don't think so,' replied Deacon. 'It was probably suffocated.'

Satisfied, Schofield handed him the forceps, then put one hand on the body's left shoulder, the other on its left hip. Gently he rolled the body towards him, allowing Deacon to take hold of the wing-tip with the forceps and gradually work the bat itself free.

Sears, watching with morbid fascination, didn't believe he'd ever seen a bat so big. It must have measured eighteen inches from the top of its round head to the tips of its clawed feet, and its wingspan was easily a metre or more. The body was covered in matted brown fur, a shade lighter on its underside. And the face! It had a high forehead and small, very black eyes that were set wide between a short, upturned snout with wide nostrils that swept back from its septum. The mouth above its jutting jaw was small, with black, leathery lips that were turned down at the edges to reveal razor-sharp incisors, beyond which he could just discern what appeared to be a long, grooved tongue. Its ears were large and almond-shaped, with a series of small ridges on the insides.

From the corner of his eye he saw Deacon deflate somehow, saw his head drop, and he said, 'This is one of yours, isn't it?'

'It's *Grande agressivo morcego*, yes,' Deacon admitted after a moment.

'So they *did* survive the winter.'

'It, ah . . . it certainly looks that way.'

'Then who does that make our friend who lived in the cellar? The one who prefers mice to McDonald's?'

Deacon stared at him. 'It's not Victor Santoro, if that's what you mean.'

'That,' Sears replied grimly, 'remains to be seen. If the DNA we get from that cellar matches whatever we can get from Santoro's belongings, you'd better rethink your opinion of your boss, Doc.'

Turning to Ryan, he said, 'Frank, I want you to dig up everything you can on Professor Victor Santoro. That's S-A-N-T-O-R-O. He was a Brazilian virologist living and working in Britain, until he disappeared about six months ago. Get me a decent photograph as well, and have it circulated to all divisions.'

Ryan nodded grimly, his eyes still fixed on the bat. 'I'll get straight onto — '

Before he could finish what he'd been saying, something entirely unexpected happened.

The dead man suddenly twitched in Schofield's grasp.

Startled, Sears and Ryan took an instinctive step away from the body. Schofield murmured, 'Good grief, he's still alive!'

And as if to prove it, the corpse made a quick, tortured, gasping sound as it drew a single, sharp breath, and then began to convulse.

Schofield grabbed the man's shoulders to hold him still and prevent further injury, but by now he was twisting and shuddering so violently that Deacon had to lend a hand, pinning the man's flailing legs as well.

Wincing with the effort of trying to hold him still, Schofield yelled, 'Well, don't just stand there, Jack! For God's sake get an ambulance! This man's still alive — and that's how we want to keep him!'

10

The minute they arrived at Edward Holcomb Hospital, Sears and Deacon were shown into a small consulting room while doctors assessed John Cooper's condition.

Deacon sank into one of the two visitor's chairs and released his breath in a low sigh. The events of the morning had left him in a daze. Paramedics had arrived at Saddler Street within minutes of the call and immediately set about trying to stabilise Cooper's condition. Only when he was heavily sedated did they begin to think about how they were going to remove him from the loft. Eventually, strapped tight to a spine board, he was lowered carefully through the hatch and taken to a waiting ambulance, which rushed him to the Acute Assessment Unit at Edward Holcomb.

What Deacon had seen of Cooper, as they lifted him into the ambulance, hadn't looked good. The big man's bitten face had appeared flushed, and vomit had started leaking from his slack mouth.

He and Sears had followed the ambulance in Sears' car, while Ryan set about instigating the various lines of enquiry Sears had outlined in the interim. Deacon himself, his mind suddenly jumbled with fear, shame and speculation, just tried to keep out of everyone's way.

'Your wife works here, doesn't she?' Sears asked suddenly.

'Yes.'

'What does she do?'

'She's a radiologist.'

Sears quirked a rare smile and said, 'I bet she sees right through *you*.'

Deacon smiled tiredly at the poor joke. But at least Sears was making an effort to put him at ease. He must know, at least within a little, just how all of this had turned Deacon's normally humdrum existence upside down. Maybe he was human after all.

Remembering the photograph he'd seen in Sears' office, Deacon said, 'What does *your* wife do?'

To his surprise, the smile suddenly vanished. 'She worked for a surveyor,' the policeman replied. '*Works*, I should say. I don't really see her anymore. We're divorced.'

'Too bad.'

Sears drew a breath, held it for a moment, then let it go with the word, 'Yeah.'

An uncomfortable silence settled after that, until Deacon asked, 'Do you want a coffee while we wait?'

'Thanks. Milk, no sugar.'

'I'll go find a machine.'

He felt a little better after he left the room. At least out here in the wide, pale green corridor, where he was anonymous amid the comings and goings of the busy hospital, he felt more able to consider what had happened and try to make sense of it all.

He was familiar with the layout of Edward Holcomb from many previous visits, and now made his way to the second floor, where the Department of Radiology was situated. In the waiting area, which was a long, windowed alcove set into one side of the corridor, he greeted an overweight receptionist called June and asked if Jan was around.

'Hello, Dr Deacon! She's up to her eyebrows at the moment, but I'll let her know you're here.'

'Thanks.'

A few minutes later, a door at the far end of the corridor opened and Jan hurried out with her white lab coat billowing around her. Deacon immediately felt a little-boy surge of relief wash through him when he saw her, though he could see from her expression that she was wondering what had brought him here and expecting it to be something bad.

'Chris!' she said with soft urgency when she was close enough. 'Is everything all right? You look terrible.'

He took her by the elbows and stood her to one side, lowering his own voice as he replied, 'I'm okay. But the killer struck again this morning. He murdered one man, and a second was attacked by bats at the same location. They're doing what they can for him right now.'

The blue eyes beneath her strawberry blonde fringe widened. 'You mean he's still *alive?*'

'Just about. But that's not the half of it. It's what else we found at the crime scene that's shaken me.'

She studied his face carefully. 'What was it?'

'A dead bat,' he said. And before she could ask the obvious question, he added, 'Yes. One of ours.'

'Are you sure?'

'It's *got* to be.'

'But I thought you said — '

'I know, I know. I didn't see any possible way they could survive a British winter. But it looks like I was wrong.'

'You can't blame yourself for that.'

'I can't *not* blame myself. I made a bad call, and because of that four people have died. Four people that we *know* of. Besides, there's more.'

'These two men I just told you about, they were attacked in an empty house. In the cellar, the police found evidence to show that someone had been living rough there for the past few weeks, and I *do* mean rough.' He hesitated, then said, 'Sears thinks it's Victor.'

'*What?*'

'I hope to God he's wrong, but I've got a terrible feeling that he might be right. And I feel awful about *that*, too.'

Jan glanced around. 'Look, come and sit down in my office for a moment.'

'I can't. Sears is waiting for me downstairs. I just needed to get it all out of my system.'

She offered him a tight smile. 'Did it help?'

'Not really. But I feel better, just seeing you.'

She made a sympathetic clucking sound, then reached out to take his arms and knead his biceps gently. 'Try not to take it personally, Chris. We don't have all the facts yet. You're blaming yourself when there probably isn't any need.'

'Maybe,' he replied without much conviction. 'Anyway, I'd better go. There's no telling how things are going to work out today, so I'll see you when I see you tonight. In the meantime, I'll text you as soon as I know what's happening.'

She reached up and pecked his cheek. 'Don't worry,' she whispered.

He went back downstairs, still telling himself that he should have guessed that something was wrong months ago. All those times he'd caught Victor just staring out of the laboratory window, or muttering distractedly to himself. He'd begun to suspect that Victor had been pushing himself too hard for too long, that he might be heading for a nervous breakdown. But he hadn't said a word about it, not even to Victor himself. And to mention it to the facility director would have been too much like telling tales out of school. Besides, if word got out that Victor was unfit for his work, he'd be finished. The scientific community was like that. No-one would ever entrust him with work of such importance again, if they suspected that he was, as Sergeant Ryan had so succinctly put it, a Person of Questionable Mental Stability.

Still, perhaps Jan was right. Maybe he *was* jumping to conclusions. DNA tests would confirm whether or not Victor and the occupant of the cellar were one and the same.

There'd be plenty of time to beat himself up then.

★ ★ ★

Forty minutes later the consulting room door swung open and a small, dark man with a face like a frog swept in. He was in his late forties, and wore his short, dark hair in a Caesar cut. He looked from one of them to the other, then said, 'Inspector Sears?'

Sears stood up. 'I'm Sears. This is Dr Deacon. He's helping with our enquiry.'

'I'm Dr Glenn,' said the physician, acknowledging Deacon's presence with a nod.

'How's the patient?' asked Sears, sitting down again.

'Dying.'

'Is he conscious? Can he talk?'

Glenn gave him a hard look. 'He can barely even draw *breath*,' he replied. 'Now, I'm going to need a list of everyone who came into contact with this man, and

I'm going to need it quickly. Can you get one made up for me? And arrange for me to screen everyone on it?'

Sears frowned. 'Yes, I can do that. But why?'

'Because unless I'm very much mistaken — and I don't believe I am — Mr Cooper appears to have contracted one of the Ebola viruses.'

Sears' voice dropped to a whisper. 'You're joking.'

'As I understand it, he was showing signs of rash, fever and nausea even as he was being removed from the, ah, scene of the crime. While I was examining him he began bleeding as well.'

'From his wounds, you mean?' asked Sears.

'No. From his mouth, his nose, his eyes and his anus.'

'Oh, Christ.'

Glenn went around his desk and dropped into the chair behind it. 'Anyway,' he said tiredly, turning his attention to Deacon now, 'I've ordered all the usual tests — a streptozyme, CBC, chemistry panel, urinalysis, VDRL, serial blood cultures and so on — and I'll be sending everything on to the National Protection Agency for confirmation, but I'm pretty sure what they're going to say.'

Deacon shook his head. 'With respect, Doctor, it can't be Ebola. Ebola has a two-to-four day incubation period. Cooper was only bitten this morning.'

'I can't comment on that. But as I'm sure you're aware, there are five distinct strains of Ebola that we know about. Maybe this is a sixth. A mutation that kills its host even more efficiently.'

'Or maybe he contracted the virus last week sometime,' suggested Deacon. 'Before he was bitten by the bats.'

'It's possible,' allowed Sears. 'We can check his movements, anyway. He must have kept a log of the jobs he went out on. But you already know how I feel about coincidence.'

He turned his attention back to Glenn. 'How can we contain this, Doctor?'

Glenn made a placating gesture with his hands. 'I don't think we should hit the panic button just yet. Fortunately, Ebola isn't an airborne virus. It spreads through contact with blood and other bodily fluids, so provided all the usual protocols were observed, as I imagine they probably *were*, the chances of anyone else contracting it is hopefully remote. But I'll want to see everyone who came into contact with Mr Cooper, just in case.'

'What *about* Cooper, anyway?' asked Sears.

'We're keeping him in isolation, obviously. And we'll provide him with all the palliative care he needs. But it's not going to be easy watching him die. And he *will* die, Inspector. Very soon, I think.'

'Poor bastard,' murmured Sears.

'Quite.' Glenn picked up the phone. 'Now, if you'll excuse me,' he said, 'I have to inform the Department of Health. It'll be for them to decide whether or not we go public with this.'

* * *

As soon as they got back to Eggerton Central, Sears arranged a hasty meeting with his boss, Detective Chief Inspector Richard Palmer. It was vital that Palmer know what had happened to John Cooper, and then seek advice as to how best to handle what had suddenly become a very delicate situation. When he finally came back into the office, Ryan asked him how things had gone.

Sears scrubbed his long, sober face and eased himself into his chair. 'The Old Man agrees with us,' he sighed. 'It'll start a panic if we go public with the news that a local man has contracted Ebola. He thinks we can expect a similar reaction if we go public with the reason why. So he's going to have a word with the Home Office, see how they think we should handle it. In the meantime, he's imposing a news blackout on Cooper and his condition. Even the poor sod's next of kin don't know the full story yet. And of course, he wants us to nail this bastard, and his pet bats, faster than ever.'

Pausing, he focused on the lanky detective sergeant. 'What have you got, anyway?'

'Nothing that'll help us give the Old Man what he wants,' Ryan replied. 'The tracker dogs picked up the suspect's scent after he left Saddler Street, but they lost it at Chapel Cut. The handlers think he deliberately went into the canal to throw the dogs off. Either that or he decided to top himself. Anyway, we're having the Cut dragged right now, just in case he's still down there, but it's not looking too hopeful.'

Sears pursed his lips, turned everything over in his mind for a moment, then said, 'What did you manage to dig up on Santoro?'

Ryan took a file from his desk and opened it. 'Victor Lourenço Santoro, born Paraminas, Brazil, 3rd September 1956. Second son of a prominent steel and petrochemical magnate. Graduated from the Faculty of Medicine, University of São Paulo, in 1981, completed doctoral studies in biochemistry, worked at hospitals in Porto Velho, Salvador and Montes Ciaros. Member of the Brazilian Academy of Sciences. As a researcher, he isolated several pharmacologically active peptides — that's chains of amino acids to you and me, Guv, not that that really helps much — and as a result was instrumental in developing several cancer vaccines and treatments for hypertension.'

'In 1995 he decided to specialise in virology, moved first to France, then England. No wife, no significant relationships of any kind, and no affiliations with any political groups. MI5 ran a check on him just before he went to work for the Government and he came up clean as a whistle.'

'What about the DNA?' asked Sears.

'We took a sample from his effects and they're seeing if it matches with the stuff we found in the cellar at Saddler Street even as we speak.'

'And Deacon?'

'Examining the dead bat,' said Ryan. He put the file back on his desk and glanced up at the wall clock. It was heading towards three o'clock. 'Any refs, Guv?' he asked.

Sears considered the question. Refreshments. The idea seemed incongruous, given the gruesome discoveries of this morning. But he knew from many years' experience that a hungry man was a distracted man, and he couldn't afford distractions right now. 'Go on, then,' he replied. 'Get me a coffee and a cheese roll.'

Ryan left the office, heading for the canteen. But as Sears watched him go, he had a nasty feeling that he was going to be distracted whether he had a full stomach or not.

He looked at the phone and wondered for perhaps the millionth time whether or not to call Stephanie. As he'd told Deacon, they hadn't seen each other since the divorce, although he'd called her a few times. On those occasions, however, Stephanie had made it clear that she didn't want any more contact with him than was necessary.

Sears, though, was of a different mind. Even though he'd tried to deny it, he needed Stephanie very badly, always had and always would. But he saw now that his devotion to his job had eventually alienated her in much the same way that it had alienated his daughter, Charlie.

Even then the penny had been slow to drop, and it was only when Charlie — Charlotte Jane — had come home at the end of her first term at university that he began to understand just how badly he'd failed them.

She'd started spouting all kinds of half-baked ideas about civil liberties and social freedoms, and how the police were just the fists of a bullish government determined to make the public toe the line, and he'd laughed at her and dismissed her often comically indignant speeches as ridiculous and ill-informed. In any case, she was a student, and students were *supposed* to rebel. She'd grow out of it in time.

But she didn't. And gradually he came to realise that she'd learned to hate the police force with such a vengeance because when she was a child it had been her main rival for his affections.

That revelation had sobered him, and he'd tried, awkwardly and without much success, to make amends. But after a while the old, no-nonsense Jack had reasserted himself, and he got sick and tired of her endless tirades against his profession, a profession that had a difficult enough job to do even at the best of times, and more often than not relied on the support of the public to get it done at all. He also reminded her on more than one occasion that it was the money he earned from that same profession that had paid her way through university in the first place.

They argued constantly after that. When the police got a result, you never got a peep out of her. But when they made a cock-up, or some silly bastard was caught taking bribes or padding a drugs haul to guarantee a conviction for the pusher he'd been trying to put away, unsuccessfully, for years, you never heard the last of it.

Still, that was one of the things Charlie never seemed to grasp. Whether you liked it or not, that was how things *were* in the real world. No-one was perfect. No *thing* was perfect. So you weeded out the corruption and the questionable practices wherever and whenever you could, and reminded yourself that for every bent copper that came to light, there were always at least another fifty good ones.

When Charlie finally left university she

went to work for a controversial and frankly paranoid organisation known as the Universal Social Freedoms Network. They were always banging on about the rights of football hooligans and binge-drinkers and other 'under-represented victims' of what they called 'heavy-handed policing methods.' Often, the USFN brought private prosecutions against individual officers on behalf of the so-called 'injured' parties. They took the supermarkets to court to stop them using loyalty cards as a means of gathering personal information, and even demanded the relaxation of 'Draconian' laws on the possession of child pornography, arguing that they infringed upon the rights of certain individuals to express their sexual preferences without fear of reprisal.

The rift between father and daughter became irreparable after that, and what made things worse was Stephanie's insistence on always taking Charlie's side.

Stephanie, like Sears himself, had come from an ordinary, working-class background. But unlike Sears, she had always been in awe of so-called 'educated' people. If Charlie said a thing was so, then it *was* so.

After all, she'd been to university, she knew what she was talking about.

Poor old Jack, whose only university had been the School of Hard Knocks, apparently didn't know his arse from his elbow.

And just maybe, he thought, Stephanie shared some of that resentment towards the police force because it had taken him away from *her*, too.

He was painfully aware now that he'd played his part in the breakdown of their marriage. In those early days he'd worked long hours simply to get where he was going. And when he got there, he continued to work long hours to make sure he *stayed* there. He always tried to leave his work at the office, but more often than not it came home with him and at dinner in the evenings or just watching telly or helping Steph do the shopping at the weekend, he would be quiet and short-tempered, his mind constantly mulling over the intricacies of this case or that crime.

In the end, Stephanie took Charlie's advice and asked for a divorce. Ever the agitator, Charlie had been pushing her to do it for as long as he could remember. It was the last thing he'd wanted, of course, but it didn't seem as if he had much say in the matter anymore. Anyway, he told himself that things might even improve between them: stranger things had happened. But Stephanie had insisted upon a clean break, so that put paid to any ideas he might have entertained of reconciliation.

The last he'd heard, Stephanie was still single, and living in a flat in one of the better suburbs of Eggerton. Charlie, now shacked up with one of her USFN colleagues, had given birth to a baby boy, Andrew William, named after the father and the father's father. Jack hadn't gotten a look in there, either.

Now, thinking about John Cooper lying in that isolation ward, with the doctors keeping him as comfortable as possible while he lay there bleeding from every orifice and simply waiting to die, Sears was reminded again of the brevity and fragility of life. And because of that he wanted to call Stephanie and set things back to rights between them. But what would he say? *How are you? What are you having for supper?* And what if he called her and she said, 'Jack? Jack *who?*'

The phone rang even as he was looking at it, and he snatched it up. 'Sears.'

He was still listening to the voice at the other end of the line when Ryan came back in, balancing two polystyrene cups one on top of the other, and carrying two white paper bags. As he set their late lunch down on the desk, Sears rang off and frowned into space.

'Everything all right, Guv?' asked Ryan, taking off his jacket.

Sears shrugged and reached for his coffee. 'I really don't know,' he replied distantly. 'That was the lab. They've made a match — they *think* — between the DNA we took from Saddler Street and the sample you got from Santoro's effects.'

Ryan sat in the visitor's chair. 'What do they mean, *think?*'

Sears looked across at him. 'Apparently there's something not quite right with the Saddler Street sample. It's Santoro's

DNA, all right. But according to the laboratory, it appears to have been ever so slightly . . . altered in some way.'

'Altered?'

'Yes,' said Sears. 'Changed . . . and yet *not* changed.'

'You've lost me.'

'I think I've lost *myself*,' Sears replied. He took a sip from his cup. The coffee was hot enough to raise a blister, and he swore. 'Right,' he said, pushing thoughts of Stephanie from his mind and reaching for the phone again. 'Let's get Deacon back here and give him the happy news.'

11

Jan worked late that evening and didn't leave the hospital until almost seven. As usual it had been a demanding day, and she was dead on her feet.

Rumours had already started circulating about the patient who'd contracted one of the Ebola viruses, of course. That kind of news had a habit of spreading fast, no matter how quiet you tried to keep it. Jan heard the story whilst taking a late-afternoon break on the mezzanine floor, but refrained from comment.

Before going back to work, however, she switched her mobile phone on to get her messages and found a text from Chris awaiting her.

DNA CONFIRMS IT'S VICTOR.

It was, she decided, the worst possible news. Now he really *wasn't* going to forgive himself.

She remembered all the times he'd expressed his concerns to her that Victor was working too hard, that he should take a break, that the people upstairs were demanding results when they had no true understanding of just how painstaking and time-consuming their work really was.

When Highcroft had burned down the previous November and Victor had disappeared, both she and Chris had suspected that he might have surprised the members of some animal liberation group and been murdered or abducted.

But now it seemed that Victor had been alive all this time, albeit in hiding, and hiding within close proximity to the very same bats that had vanished from Highcroft before the fire, and had also been believed dead.

She couldn't even begin to think what it all meant, and neither did she try. Her main concern now was Chris, and how all this was going to affect him in the long run. When they caught Victor and the full story — whatever it was — came out, things were going to become very, very difficult for him.

It had been a warm day and the heat

showed no sign of dissipating as and she drove her red Peugeot 207 toward home. The early evening was calm and peaceful, the sky a clear, cloudless blue, and traffic was mercifully light. Within twenty minutes she was turning the car onto the gravel drive outside the cottage and parking just in front of the closed garage doors.

She let herself into the house, collected the mail from the cage behind the letter box and whistled for Minor, who for once hadn't come rushing to greet her with his usual frantic mixture of licks, barks and playful hand-bites.

As she went through to the kitchen, she studied the envelopes. Satisfied that most of it was routine or junk mail, she put the post on the worktop, opened the fridge and took out a jug of fresh orange juice. She had just finished pouring herself a glass when she realised that there was still no sign of Minor.

With a frown she went to the foot of the stairs and called his name. During the day he was usually happy to surround himself with his toys and crunchies, and let himself out into the garden through the cat-flap in the kitchen's Dutch door whenever he felt like a change of scene. But he could always be relied upon to be there to greet them when they got home from work — though not tonight, apparently.

Sipping her orange juice, Jan went upstairs and checked the bedrooms, fully expecting to find Minor snuggled up fast asleep on or under one of the beds.

But he was nowhere to be found.

She went back down to the kitchen and unlocked the Dutch door. It opened onto a wide patio scattered with white garden furniture. In the middle of the lawn stood a log pergola overgrown with bougainvillea, white wisteria and Blue Moon roses. Just beyond the pergola, an ivy-covered tool shed with a pitched felt roof occupied the far right-hand corner of the forty-by-thirty metre garden.

'Minor!' she called. 'Minor? Where are you, you naughty boy?'

Concern started to nag at her now. Where *had* he gone? He'd never before displayed the wanderlust she usually associated with Jack Russells, and had always preferred the comforts of home. But at the back of her mind was some half-remembered story she'd seen on television about gangs who went around stealing dogs and then demanding money for their safe return. She couldn't believe that such a thing had happened to Minor, but the events of the day had already unsettled her, and if she wasn't careful this new concern was in danger of mushrooming out of all proportion.

'*Minor!*'

There was irritation in her voice this time, but she knew that the minute she saw his little black face and chocolate-brown eyes peering out of the bushes she'd be too happy to even *consider* scolding him.

But still he failed to put in an appearance.

She bit her lower lip, not really knowing what to do for the best. Maybe she should call the local police station and see if he'd been handed in at all, though she had no idea how he could possibly have escaped from the garden in the first place. It was enclosed by a two-metre panel fence, and a tall, thick *leylandii* hedge.

As she turned and started back into the house, she thought she heard a faint whimper from somewhere behind her. Immediately she spun back to face the garden, which had now started to look increasingly gloomy in the changing light.

'Minor? Baby, is that you?'

But the silence was absolute now. Even the birds that normally inhabited the garden were hushed.

No, she realised suddenly, *not hushed*. There *are* no birds.

She wondered if she'd imagined the sound. But no — she was sure that she *had* heard it. It had come from the far end of the garden somewhere.

She set her glass down on the garden table nearby and started up the path. Again she called the dog's name, but again there was no response.

She skirted around the pergola. The myrtle bushes that enclosed it on three sides rendered the grassed area behind it more or less invisible from the house. Not that there was much to see on the far side, just another strip of lawn about four metres wide that ended in a tall, impenetrable row of *leylandii*. To her right sat the ivy-covered shed, a clutter of forks, rakes, spades and empty flowerpots just visible through its dusty windows.

It came to her then that there was a sort of secret garden to the left of the shed, although 'secret garden' was pushing it a bit. Actually, it was a constantly shady spot that no-one had ever really found a good use for, and she had always intended to clear it out, fence it off and put in some vegetables, but never quite got round to it. Minor rarely ventured into it because it held nothing of appeal to him. But maybe just this once he'd decided to explore it after all and trapped or injured himself.

With that thought in mind, she hurried to the side of the shed and scanned the cool shadows that forever congregated there. The ivy had spread everywhere, and the little corner patch smelled unpleasantly of damp, decomposing vegetation.

'Minor?' she called, moderating her tone now, just wanting him to come to her so that she could satisfy herself that he was all right.

Nothing.

All at once she felt completely, utterly alone.

But still she went a little deeper into the shadows.

'Come on, baby, it's me!'

Then she heard it again, a soft, almost desperate mixture of cry-and-growl. Minor was definitely somewhere behind the shed, maybe trapped in the narrow gap between the shed and the hedge that ran alongside it.

Urgently now she pushed a path through tall weeds and old cobwebs, making for the far corner of the shed. 'Come on, baby,' she called.

A moment later she reached the corner.

And froze.

A man was standing there, waiting for her. A man who wasn't a man at all, with Minor struggling frantically to escape from beneath his left arm.

Their eyes met. Hers were wide. The eyes of the man-thing were an insane, glittering black.

Then, before she could scream, he dropped the dog, lunged at her and his right hand — claw — clamped hard across her mouth, and almost before she knew it, she was *his*.

* * *

At eight-thirty Deacon parked his midnight-blue Auris in the lay-by opposite the cottage and killed the engine. Beyond the windscreen, the sky was slowly fading from steel blue to slate grey.

He sat there for a few moments, just listening to the ticking of the engine as it cooled, and reviewing the events of the afternoon.

He couldn't say that the news about Victor had come as much of a surprise. All day long he'd been coming round to the idea that Victor and the man in the cellar really *were* one and the same. He didn't know what had brought Victor to such a sorry state and couldn't even begin to speculate, but no matter how much he'd braced himself for it, the news had still hit him hard.

'What I don't get,' Sears went on, 'is this anomaly they've found in the DNA. According to the lab, it's Santoro's DNA, all right, but it's been *distorted* somehow. Any ideas, Doc?'

Still struggling to absorb the fact that a man he'd believed dead was actually still alive, Deacon had had to force himself to concentrate. 'It's not really my field,' he muttered weakly.

'No,' said Sears, 'I suppose not. We'll just have to ask him when we catch him, won't we?'

'Your men are sure he didn't drown in Chapel Cut, then?'

'Positive. But where he went after he climbed out again is anyone's guess.'

'Monk's Tunnel?'

'We checked. He didn't even go near it.'

Just then the phone rang and Sears snatched it up. He listened for a few moments, then said, 'All right. Thanks, Doctor. Yes, we will.'

He replaced the receiver, then looked from Deacon to Ryan. 'That was Dr Glenn at Edward Holcomb,' he said.

'John Cooper died about ten minutes ago.'

Ryan whistled. 'Bloody hell, that was quick.'

'*Too* quick,' declared Deacon. 'Ebola kills quickly, but not *that* quickly. A week, perhaps. Maybe two. But not in less than twelve hours.' He considered the situation for a moment. 'Are you *sure* Cooper couldn't have been scratched or bitten and infected sometime last week?'

'We've checked his log,' said Ryan. 'He carried out a few cockroach treatments, cleaned and serviced the Insect-o-cutors for a local supermarket and baited a caravan park and a local brewery for rats — part of a regular maintenance contract he had, not because the rats have suddenly started making a comeback — and that was all. According to his next of kin, he was in good health, didn't complain of any injuries.'

'What have you managed to find out about the dead bat?' asked Sears.

'I'm still waiting for the results of the tests I ran this afternoon, and I have a few more to conduct tomorrow. But so far, nothing to confirm that it was carrying a new strain of Ebola, I'm afraid.'

He stopped suddenly, as a new thought struck him. Sears, noticing it, said, 'What's up?'

'I'm not really sure.'

'Well let's hear it, anyway.'

Deacon looked from Sears to Ryan and back again. Haltingly, he said, 'It's generally believed that most outbreaks of Ebola are self-limiting for the very simple reason that the virus kills its host so quickly, thus limiting its opportunity to spread. That's especially true of, say, the Zaire Ebola virus, which has a kill-rate in excess of ninety percent.'

'Though this 'self-limiting' idea is largely erroneous, however, there is one element of truth to it. The virus does die with the host.'

'Meaning . . . ?' prompted Sears.

'Meaning John Cooper was the only victim so far who didn't have his head smashed in,' said Deacon.

Sears thought about that. 'Are you telling me that Santoro has been braining these people in order to kill the virus before it has a chance to spread?'

'I think I am, yes.'

'That's crazy.'

'Yes. But so is Victor, apparently. Perhaps in his way he's trying to spare his victims as much suffering as possible. Or maybe he's doing it to . . . I don't know . . . to limit the damage for the rest of us.'

'It's possible, I suppose,' Sears allowed grudgeingly. 'But what concerns me now is where this thing goes from *here*. We can't keep a lid on it indefinitely. We've already got the parents of Catherine Weller threatening to go to the papers unless we tell them the full story. Cooper's lot'll start up as well, now that he's dead. But if we tell 'em the truth, and they spill it to anyone else, we've got a panic on our hands.'

'You can't *not* tell them,' argued Deacon. 'They have a right to know. The *public* has a right to know, to protect itself.'

'That's for the DCI and the Home Office to decide,' growled Sears. 'In the meantime, maybe the autopsy'll throw some light on why the virus killed Cooper so quickly.'

He glanced at Deacon, saw how haggard he looked and said, 'You might as well go home, Doc. You're no good to me if you're dead on your feet.'

Deacon gave him a crooked smile and said without rancour, 'You're all heart, Inspector.'

Now, as he finally climbed out of the car and started across the quiet country lane, Deacon noticed two things which made him frown. Jan's car was nowhere to be seen, and the cottage itself was in darkness.

He let himself inside, shrugged out of his jacket and hung it on the rack.

'Jan?' he called.

There was no response.

He went through to the kitchen and switched on the lights. He realised then that there was no sign of Minor, either. His basket, in the corner beside the refrigerator, was empty. Maybe Jan had taken him for a walk.

But why is her car missing?

He went upstairs, still preoccupied by the events of the day, stripped off and took a shower. The hot water felt good, but failed to calm the persistent feeling of foreboding within him.

He towelled himself dry, put on his dressing gown and went back downstairs. There was still no sign of Jan or Minor. He checked the wall-clock in the kitchen. It was a little after nine. The country roads were lethal for pedestrians after dark, and Jan knew it. But maybe she'd run into a talkative neighbour she hadn't been able to break away from.

It was possible. But of course, it *still* didn't explain why her car was missing.

He went to the sink in order to fill the kettle. His reflection in the window showed him dark-ringed eyes in a face tight with worry.

And beyond his reflection —

At first he thought his eyes were deceiving him. But *no*. There *was* something vague and indistinct cowering in the middle of the lawn.

He switched off the tap, set the kettle aside and hurried to the Dutch door. To his surprise, he found it unlocked. He opened it and went out onto the patio.

In the gloom he could see it more clearly. He called, '*Minor?*'

173

The dog was watching him from a distance of seven or eight metres, his floppy black ears down, his tail tucked between his legs. He was shivering.

Deacon hurried across the grass. 'Hey! Come on, boy, what's wrong?'

The dog watched him come from the corner of one eye, a sheepish, almost apologetic expression on his lowered head. Deacon bent, scooped the animal up and glanced around. 'Jan?'

But they were all alone.

He turned and started to carry Minor inside. When he drew level with the garden table, he saw that a nearly-full glass of orange juice had been left there. Frowning, he continued inside, set the dog down on the slate floor and gave him a brief examination. He wasn't injured at all, but clearly spooked.

Why?

Deacon hurried into the hallway and took his mobile phone from his jacket pocket. He went back into the kitchen and was just about to call Jan's number when he noticed a scrap of paper sitting on the worktop, beside that day's mail.

He must have missed it earlier.

He took his glasses from his dressing gown pocket and put them on. The note had been written on paper torn from the pad they kept by the phone in the hallway. It said, in Jan's handwriting:

WAIT. I WILL CALL.

As he took the glasses off again, his frown deepened. *Wait?* What was that supposed to mean? Wait for *what?*

He glanced at Minor again. The dog was standing exactly where Deacon had left him, looking positively sick with nerves. Something bad had happened here, something that had thrown a terrible scare into him. But *wha* —

Suddenly the phone in his hand buzzed, and he was so startled that he almost dropped it. A moment later, he said eagerly, 'Hello, Jan?'

Silence.

'Jan? Are you there?'

And then —

' . . . Chris . . . ?'

He felt almost light-headed with relief. '*Jan!* Where are you, I've been — '

'C-Chris, please. Just listen.'

He caught it then, the high-wire strain in her voice, the tight, scared tone of it, and began to feel sick with nerves himself. 'Are you all right?' he asked urgently. 'What's happened?'

'Please, Chris! Just . . . just listen. *Please*.'

'All right, all right, I'm listening.'

He heard the sound she made swallowing at the other end of the line. 'Y-you've got to come to F-Fenady Street,' she said. 'Do you know it?'

'No, but the sat nav will. What's — '

'Come *now*,' she interrupted. 'B-bring a flashlight and . . . yes, all right!'

He realised with a start that she was addressing someone who was at the other end of the line with her. Then:

'And c-come alone. You *must* come alone, Chris.'

'Jan,' he said. 'What's *happened?*'

'H-he's here,' she said, and had to give vent to a constricted sort of sob and swallow before she could say any more. 'And h-he wants to speak to you.'

Deacon shook his head. '*Who* wants to speak to me?' he asked.

'*V-Victor*,' she replied in a whisper.

12

Deacon punched the address into the sat nav with unsteady fingers and followed the subsequent directions with only half an ear. His mind was still reeling from the shock of what Jan had said, that she was with Victor, that Victor wanted to see him.

Victor!

He hadn't even considered calling Sears. Jan had told him he had to come alone, and he would, if that's what it took to keep her safe.

He'd dressed hastily in jeans and a tee-shirt, grabbed the flashlight from the shelf under the staircase and, with one final stroke for Minor, hurried out to the car, where he programmed the satellite navigation system and then drove back towards Eggerton. According to the sat nav, Fenady Street was on the east side of the city, not far from Monk's Tunnel and the scene of Terry Marsh's murder.

As the country lanes eventually yielded

to the more built-up suburbs, and finally to the outskirts of Eggerton itself, he tried to piece everything together. It seemed safe to assume that Victor had somehow managed to abduct Jan in order to force him to do as he said, and that Minor had witnessed the abduction and that was what had traumatised him. But what did Victor want? *Help?* Maybe. And Deacon would give it, gladly, so long as it guaranteed Jan's safety.

He glanced at his watch. It was a little after ten. He had no idea where the time had gone. The empty streets were dark now but for the dull mustard glow of the neon streetlights, and as he drew closer to Fenady Street, which was located in a run-down area that had been awaiting regeneration for years now, they grew darker and emptier still.

At last he reached his destination. It was an old-fashioned cobbled cul-de-sac flanked by tall, slum-like structures that were now empty and awaiting demolition. In years gone by these had probably been factories, sweat-shops and warehouses, the area itself a hive of activity. Now it was just a haven for rats — or *would* be, if the rats hadn't already cleared out.

He spotted Jan's Peugeot up ahead and parked in front of it. He took the flashlight, got out of the car, hurried back to the Peugeot and looked inside. It was empty.

He walked back to the Auris, flashed his headlights a couple of times, then switched off the engine and waited for some sort of response. Darkness draped itself across the street, filling every peeling doorway and boarded-up window, and even though the night was humid, he shivered.

One minute turned into ten, then fifteen, then twenty-five. Deacon's eyes began to ache with the strain of just watching. He thought perhaps he would try to call Jan back, but even as he reached for his phone a movement caught his eye, and he saw that one of the shadows at the far end of the street had detached itself from the rest.

His stomach muscles tensed unpleasantly. All he could see from this distance was a pale oval of face, a tall, slim body, black trousers streaked to the knees with mud or dirt, and with a kind of desperation he mouthed the name, *Jan*.

Then he saw that a second, smaller figure was standing behind and a little to one side of her, one hand, the right one, grasping Jan tightly by her hair. The two of them stepped down into the kerb, and then the second figure — it could only be Victor — raised his free hand and waved him forward.

Drawing a deep breath, Deacon scooped the flashlight off the roof of the Auris, where he'd left it, and started walking towards them, his pulses racing.

The distance between them halved, and it became a little easier to make out Jan's pale face and the big, scared eyes that sat within it. As he came closer, his eyes locked with hers and with them he tried to say, *Don't worry. I'm here now. It'll be all right.*

Then Victor, still largely hidden behind his hostage, the rest of him indistinct in the darkness, raised his free hand again and Deacon, anxious to cooperate, immediately came to a halt. They stood frozen then, all three of them.

'Victor?' he called at last.

For a long moment there was silence. Then a low, rasping voice that was and yet wasn't Victor's, said, 'You came . . . alone?'

It made Deacon's skin crawl to hear it. 'Of course.'

He took a pace forward, but the movement made Victor's silhouette stiffen, and he stopped again. 'Victor, please. I'm here now. Let Jan go. *Yes?*'

That low, sibilant voice came again. 'In time.'

'Well . . . what is it that you want? I'll do whatever I can, if you'll only — '

'Talk,' said the shadowy figure, the effort of forming the words clearly a strain. '*Explain*. And then . . . y-you help.'

Deacon bobbed his head eagerly. 'That's good, Victor. We'll talk. All I ask is that — '

'But not . . . here,' grated Victor. And as he backed up a little, the shadows thrown by a streetlamp off to his left finally slid away from his face, and Deacon saw him properly for the first time.

He thought, *My God*.

His eyes stung at the sight before him. 'Victor,' he almost choked. 'What happened?'

Victor was a wreck. He had lost weight, was stooped, grubby and whiskery. He wore soiled black trousers and a once-white shirt, both of them now stained, creased, torn and stiff with dried blood-marks. His black hair, which before had always been so neatly barbered, was now long, unkempt and matted, and stuck behind the belt he wore at his emaciated waist Deacon saw the hammer with which he had already killed at least four people.

But it was in his face itself where the change was most evident. As Deacon studied him, he had the weirdest feeling that his eyes were playing tricks on him, for Victor's features appeared to have been *stretched* somehow, or perhaps *remoulded* was a more accurate description. The forehead was ever so slightly higher than he remembered, the eyes set just a little wider apart. Victor's nose seemed somehow flatter, more snubbed, the nostrils reformed so that in the poor light they appeared more like black teardrops that had been tipped onto their sides.

His mouth, too, had changed. The lips were darker, thinner, and they turned down at the corners to give him a belligerent aspect.

Victor moved quickly to put himself back into shadow. He made no reply, just motioned with his free, misshapen hand that Deacon should go ahead of him.

Deacon did so, speculating now on whether or not he could take Victor by surprise, use the flashlight as a weapon, get Jan away from him and make it back to the car.

But then he thought about John Cooper, and how quickly the man had died. A single wound from Victor, even the smallest scratch, might mean a painful death for he and Jan both, and that made it a risk he couldn't take.

Besides — and here he glanced up and around him, his skin seeming to shrink across his skull at the very notion — what if the bats were roosting nearby, watching their every move?

He walked on ahead until he came to what appeared to be a narrow alleyway that was closed off by a heavy, rusted iron gate. Once the gate had been fastened shut by an equally heavy padlock, but apparently Victor's hammer had made short work of that, for it now hung loose and broken at the end of its thick chain.

Deacon slowed until, behind him, Victor said in his hissing, bubbly voice, 'Open it.'

Deacon did, and went through into the darkness beyond. 'Can I use the torch now?' he asked without turning his head.

There came a grunt that he took to mean yes.

He switched the flashlight on. Its beam showed him an alleyway two metres wide and thirty metres long, flanked on either side by a tall, crumbling brown-brick wall across which grew patches of green mould. At the far end of the alley, a manhole cover had been removed from the manhole itself.

'Move,' grated Victor.

But Jan held back, and when he glanced around at her, Deacon saw that she was shaking her head, trying to mouth something with tremulous lips, and in her eyes was pure terror.

'I *can't*,' she almost whimpered. 'I can't. Not again.'

Deacon said, 'Victor — '

'Move,' rasped Victor.

'But Jan's — '

'*Move!*' snapped Victor, and with a sudden, prolonged hiss he shoved Jan forward into Deacon's arms, his head sank into his shoulders and his right hand/claw ripped the hammer from the belt and lifted it high. The dark lips peeled back, showing a glimpse of sharp, decaying teeth as the angry hiss went on and on —

Deacon quickly fumbled Jan behind him, shone the flashlight full into Victor's face, and suddenly Victor was backing off, flustering in his haste to get out of the beam of light.

'All right, Victor! All right! Just calm dow — '

The words died in his throat then, as he got a better look at the other man.

Oh Christ . . .

Victor's eyes had always been dark. Now they were like two lumps of wet coal, all dilated pupil and little else. And the stubble on his cheeks and chin . . . he saw now that it wasn't stubble at all.

Victor's face was covered in a fine scraping of sleek, glossy brown *fur*.

'Victor . . . '

The compassion in his voice made Victor suddenly freeze and stare at him. Gradually the fury in his black eyes seemed to fade. His lids flickered several times, and then the anger drained from him altogether.

'Go,' he said in his scratchy voice.

Shaken, Deacon turned to Jan, squeezed her arm. 'It'll be all right,' he whispered.

Together they walked slowly down to the manhole, Jan having to be coaxed all the way. The only sound was the reluctant shuffle of their steps on the powdery concrete screed underfoot. When they reached the edge of the hole, they stopped again.

'Down,' said Victor.

Deacon shone the torch into the manhole. It was a little over a metre in diameter. A rusted wrought-iron ladder was attached to the far wall. It dropped into a foul-smelling darkness that not even the torchlight could penetrate.

Carefully, Deacon lowered himself into the hole and began to descend, rung by corroded rung. After a moment Jan followed on, and behind her came Victor.

For a long time there was nothing but the uncertain to and fro of the flashlight, the echo and clatter of their feet on the cold rungs, and their heavy breathing. Deacon tried to gauge how deep the manhole was. It was almost impossible to guess, but at least ten metres, maybe a little more.

The ladder ended so suddenly that he almost fell backwards as he stepped down into nothing save cold water.

He gave an involuntary cry of surprise, righted himself, quickly inspected their surroundings by flashlight.

He was standing in a wide brick tunnel, thigh-deep in murky water the colour of green olives. The smell of damp and decay made him want to puke.

He reached up to help Jan down from the ladder, held her to him while he could, squeezed her, whispered, 'Are you all right?'

'Y . . . yes.'

'Well, just hold on. Everything'll be — '

Then Victor, a shrunken, twisted shadow against darker shadows, dropped into the sewer beside them with a light splash, and he fell silent again.

'There,' said Victor, and pointed briefly with the claw still holding the hammer. 'Go . . . there.'

Deacon and Jan exchanged a glance. She was in shock and trying to fight it, her mascara-smudged eyes frighteningly vacant. 'Victor, there's no need for — '

'There is *every* . . . need.'

Deacon hesitated a moment more, then took Jan's left hand, and together they began to wade in the direction Victor had indicated.

By torchlight, he saw that the sewer had a curved roof. Off-white deposits of fat, oil and grease glistened everywhere. The smell was stronger now, and there could be no ignoring the awful, unmistakable stink of human waste that surrounded them.

Victor kept them wading forward. Gradually the floor of the tunnel began to dip, the cloudy water through which they were struggling to climb close to waist-height. Deacon, feeling and fumbling his way forward, his every sense heightened by an unshakable sense of dread, started to feel claustrophobic and short of breath. Glancing up, he saw a ragged water-mark staining the bricks near the top of the tunnel, and found it easy to imagine what this sewer would be like in full flood.

Then Victor grunted something and he realised that they had come to a heavy iron door in the left-side wall, a thick, mottled and oxidized thing of lozenge-shape which could only be reached by climbing a flight of five worn steps, and could only be opened — perhaps *unsealed* was a better word — by turning a rusted wheel at its centre. Deacon looked at Victor. Victor made a rough, impatient gesture.

'Open it,' he ordered in his chafing voice.

Deacon handed the flashlight to Jan, took hold of the flaking wheel. At first he thought it was stuck fast, but then, with a protesting wrench of sound that echoed like a scream along the tunnel, it suddenly gave. Deacon turned it, heard strap-iron bolts slide back, top and bottom, from the other side.

'Go . . . through,' rasped Victor.

Deacon pulled the door open, took the flashlight back and shone it into the room beyond.

At first glance he thought it might be some kind of storeroom. It was perhaps ten metres long and five metres wide, built from smooth, red-orange bricks, with a dusty concrete floor. To left and right, three pipes followed the wall-floor junction to the far end, big, grey cylinders bolted securely into place. The right-side pipe was massive, easily a metre and a half wide. A smaller pipe had been bolted or welded along the top. In the facing wall he saw a second heavy iron door, also of the same distinctive shape.

He stepped inside. His footsteps echoed softly and caused a brief fluttering sound overhead.

At once he swung the flashlight up so

that it played over the high ceiling. Clinging to a network of pipes, cables and switched-off strip lights twenty metres above them, hanging upside down and wrapped tightly in their own dark, vein-lined wings, were a cluster of large bats, too many to count at once, but certainly more than forty.

He felt Jan grab his free arm, and he pulled her close. He looked up at the bats, some swaying gently, others stirring or flexing, still more making low chattering sounds, and remembering what they were capable of, he felt another shiver run through him.

'Wh — '

His throat was so dry that speech had suddenly become an effort.

'What now, Victor?' he managed at last.

'Now,' said Victor, closing the door behind him and turning the wheel to seal them all in. 'Now I am g-going to . . . tell you about the bats. What they . . . want.'

'And what they will do if they don't get it.'

13

But even before the words had left his lips, Victor's expression turned vague, almost lost. Again Deacon and his wife exchanged a glance. Then Deacon said gently, 'Victor?'

Victor blinked, seemed to realise that he'd been elsewhere for those few short seconds, and said softly, '*Como? Não compreendo . . .*'

'You were going to tell us about the bats, Victor. About what happened.'

A frown creased Victor's high forehead. 'What happened?' he repeated, as if the words were a puzzle to him.

Deacon drew breath and spoke again, softly, for fear of disturbing the bats. 'Yes, Victor. About the bats. About what happened at Highcroft.'

Victor walked past them, leaving smudgy wet footprints in his wake, and flopped down against the massive pipe, a man/thing exhausted beyond measure.

'Yes,' he croaked, finally tucking the hammer back into his belt. 'Yes. Highcroft.'

He paused momentarily, then said, 'I can't truly . . . explain what happened, or why. P-perhaps it was because I had . . . worked so often with them . . . in the past, b-both in Brazil and France. Perhaps I built a . . . bond with the species. But I was never aware of that at any time. N-not until we s-set to work at Highcroft.'

'Even now I don't know exactly when it . . . began. I suppose it started as a vague . . . sensation. Like hearing voices in a room next door. Half-heard, half . . . understood. But strange, because you know that the room next door is empty and that . . . n-no-one should be in there speaking at all.'

'At first I dismissed it as . . . imagination. That I was over-tired. But as the days went by, I grew more and more . . . convinced that something was . . . talking to me. Trying to *communicate* with me.'

'The bats?' hazarded Deacon.

Victor nodded. 'They were reaching

out . . . trying to . . . *speak* to me,' he said. The large black eyes caught something in Deacon's face and he said irritably, 'Oh, not with words. Not with . . . *language*, as such. Images. Pictures. No, not even those. *Colours, feelings, shapes.* Things that conveyed emotions and ideas to me.'

'Of . . . course, I feared for my sanity at first, t-tried to . . . b-block it out, pretend that it . . . wasn't happening. But there was no escaping it. Even . . . when I left the laboratory at night or at . . . week-ends, I could still see or sense the images in my mind, hear that cease . . . ceaseless chattering. The rainforest, the sounds of its birds and the colours of its snakes, lizards, leopards and jaguars . . . its warmth and humidity, a world of tall, moss-covered trees and low, drifting . . . cloud. I felt . . . I *experienced* them all.'

'But there was sadness in those images, C-Christopher. A longing, a *need*, to go back there. To go *home*. It went on and on and on and there w-was nothing I could do to stop it.'

'I could tell you that they . . . wore me down, eventually. And perhaps in a way they *did*. But I also came to understand and *sympathise* with their plight. They h-hadn't . . . asked to come here. They were t-torn from their home and th-thrust into a sterile laboratory environment, for *our* convenience and *our* benefit. Once I . . . understood that, it f-finally dawned upon me that th-they wanted . . . to go home. And that they wanted me to b-be the one to *take* them home.'

'Of course, I had no . . . idea how I would do that, and I . . . told them so, making a feeble . . . attempt to communicate with them in their own . . . w-way. B-but I also told them that I would do . . . everything I could, and after that the visions eased, the constant, maddening chatter ceased, and I was allowed some m-measure of peace.'

'I t-tried to work out how the thing could be done . . . legitimately. I thought that, once we had c-concluded our research, I could request that the b-bats be returned home. S-say, as a goodw-will gesture, to placate the animal liberation p-people. B-but the research took too long, the b-bats grew impatient and the . . . the images and endless chattering began to cloud my thinking again.'

'Eventually I decided that I w-would have to steal them away, h-hide them in my flat until it was . . . safe for us to m-make our move. I thought perhaps that af-after a few months there might be a . . . a way that I could buy passage aboard a ship and return to Brazil by sea. After all, I h-had money. Enough to ensure that th-there would be no . . . questions asked about my . . . cargo.'

'S-so one night I stayed late at work, and transferred all the bats from their cases into three holdalls.' He gave a short, high laugh that made the bats above them stir restlessly. 'H-hold-alls!' he repeated derisively. 'B-but they came willingly, because they knew . . . that I was doing what they wanted, that I was *obeying* them.'

'I carried them out to my car, set them down on the back seat, went back to the laboratory and set fire to the place in order . . . to destroy any sign of what I had done, and m-make the police believe that . . . one of the animal liberation g-groups had freed the bats and destroyed the . . . lab.'

Suddenly he frowned. 'But even then my thinking was . . . impaired,' he went on. 'After it was done, I w-was seized by panic, afraid that I would break down under police questioning or th-that they would want to search my flat and discover what I had done. S-so I decided to d-disappear with the bats, and I . . . I did.'

'I drove us to my . . . flat, c-collected food, some clothes and blankets, and then l-left town. I d-drove until I found a secluded spot in the m-middle of nowhere, hidden by trees and, fr-from the looks of it, seldom visited, and we . . . stayed there for a while. I needed . . . time to plan wh-what we were going to do next, h-how we were going to return to Brazil, b-but the bats, in th-their impatience, had forced m-me to act too soon. It was already winter, too cold for them to h-have any hope of survival. B-by then, however, it w-was too late. Th-there was . . . no turning back.'

He looked up suddenly, fixing Deacon with a sharp, animate expression. The flashlight threw shadows up over his bat-face, giving it an even eerier appearance, and the shadow of his head and shoulders loomed large behind him.

'And yet they *d-did* survive, Christopher! Over a period of . . . days, I began to notice a ch-change in them. Their body temperatures dropped, their heart rates decreased, th-their breathing slowed. They entered a deep state or torpor, so deep that it was a . . . long time before I realised they weren't in fact . . . d-dying. Their metabolic rate dropped to almost nothing, and th-they slept.'

'For *months*, they slept, with me watching over them. The car was . . . our world now. B-but I knew we couldn't stay there in . . . definitely. And when I had used up the last of my . . . supplies, I had . . . no option b-but to drive us back into Eggerton and . . . g-go in search of a . . . s-safer, warmer location in which to await the s-spring.'

198

'At first I f-found a c-collapsed t-tunnel. It had c-collapsed years earlier, m-marking the end of a canal that once ran through it. B-but if one was willing to t-take the risk, there was a w-way into its darkest depths. S-so I took the bats there, dumped m-my car in an even poorer part of town and l-left it f-for thieves to steal or vandals to wreck. And . . . b-because the tunnel was s-so close to the sh-shops, I w-was free to forage throughout the hours of darkness in order to keep myself from starving.'

'I lived on what little I could find in bins outside takeaways, on what rotten fruit was left . . . behind after th-the market traders had gone for the day. L-later still, I learned to live on . . . o-other things.'

Deacon thought about the tiny bones they'd found in the cellar at Saddler Street, and wanted to be sick.

'In . . . evitably, h-however, I grew weak, lost weight. But still I watched over the bats, for even though they were in a state of torpor they were still with me, in here.' He tapped his too-high forehead. 'And somehow the months passed, albeit in a sort of h-haze for me, until eventually, o-over a period of days, the bats began to stir again.'

'Five died during that period of . . . hibernation. Just five, from a colony of fifty. The rest woke up hungry and f-filled with the desire to . . . hunt, and they went in search of prey. They hunted rats at first, until the rats eventually grew wise to them and w-went to ground.'

'It was th-then that it . . . happened,' he said, and abruptly fell silent, a faraway look returning to his black eyes.

Deacon licked his lips. '*What* happened, Victor?' he asked carefully.

The black eyes sharpened again. 'E-even bats as . . . asocial as *Grande agressiva morcego* sh-share certain . . . traits, similarities, with other, less . . . confrontational species. Th-they cluster together for warmth and security, and just like m-many bats, they are capable of sur-surprising acts of . . . altruism.'

'You've heard of bats . . . regurgitating blood-meals for those in their colonies not able to feed for themselves?'

'Of course.'

'Th-that is what they did for *me*.'

'*What?*'

'B-by the time they woke up, I was . . . sick, mal . . . nourished, close, I think, to death. The bats saw that and . . . b-began to regurgitate blood-meals for me. I had no choice but to . . . accept them. And in time I grew strong enough to . . . look after myself again, to move them to an even b-better location, an empty house not far from the tunnel. By then, however . . . the damage had been done.'

'S-something in the blood-meals — p-perhaps a reaction of enzymes, or possibly my body's natural r-response to the haemoparasites common in all bats — began to . . . change me. Subtly, at first, but then more pro . . . foundly. My senses became *heightened*, somehow. My vision, my h-hearing . . . it was as if I were r-reborn. B-but I also grew light-sensitive, lost the enamel on my incisors . . . '

Deacon swallowed softly, remembering the findings which suggested that Victor's DNA had been distorted in a way that no-one could explain.

'And I . . . b-became the thing you see before you now,' Victor croaked.

His head dropped, his claw/hands flexed and relaxed, flexed and relaxed.

It was a moment before Deacon realised he was crying.

'We'll help you, Victor,' he said gently. 'Somehow, we'll set things back to rights.'

But Victor shook his head. 'No going back,' he husked, and Deacon had the feeling that he was voicing a thought that had played through his mind many times more than once. 'Too late now. Too many people dead. Too many people . . . still to die.'

'What was that?'

Victor raised his head again. '*Como?*'

'What did you mean, 'too many people still to die'?'

Victor shook his head, confused and trying to bring order to his thoughts. 'At first the bats were . . . content to hunt rodents,' he explained. 'And when they fled, they turned their attention to birds, pigeons mostly . . . th-then animals. Stray cats, dogs. Animals we f-found in a local zoo.'

'But I was always *fearful*, Christopher. Always . . . fearful. The bats carried the very . . . filoviruses w-we h-had been hoping to combat. I-if they were to *spread* those viruses . . . '

It was, then, as Deacon had suspected. He gestured towards the hammer at Victor's waist and said, 'So you decided to kill their victims, in the hope that the virus, if it *was* passed on, would die with the new host.'

Victor swallowed. He made another quick, restless gesture. 'Y-yes. But perhaps I wasn't . . . thinking clearly at that point.'

Victor hadn't been thinking clearly at *any* point, but Deacon let that pass. 'Go on,' he said.

'What else is there . . . to say? The animals . . . they weren't *enough*. They didn't p-provide enough . . . *sport* . . . for the bats. Th-their naturally aggressive temperament demanded something m-more. And the only prey that . . . remained . . . were *humans*. The hated humans who had . . . taken them from the rainforest and brought them here in the first place. B-besides, there was . . . another reason.'

'Which was?' prodded Deacon, when Victor made no move to continue.

'To provide an example of what they could . . . and *would* do, if their demands were not met.'

This time it was Deacon who shook his head. 'I don't understand,' he said.

'They want to go . . . *home*, Christopher. *I* want to go home. And the bats will give me no peace until I *take* them home! But how am I to do that, now? I can't. I can't do it alone.'

Deacon felt his skin tingling again. 'Are you asking me to *help* you?' he whispered.

Victor said, 'Yesss . . . '

'But, Victor — I *can't!* What you were proposing to do, what you say the bats *wanted* you to do . . . it was *never* going to happen! Do you *really* think you could have left this country undetected? Do you think Brazil would allow you all back in, after what's happened? People have *died*, Victor! And the police are already onto you! It's only a matter of time before they track you down!'

Victor's face creased into a snarl and that awful, sibilant hiss escaped from between his leathery lips again. Above them, the bats began to chatter in clear agitation. Two of them dropped from their roosting spots and began fluttering angrily around the high ceiling before settling again.

'Never . . . theless,' Victor said, calming himself after a moment, 'it must be . . . done. The bats will settle for nothing less. And they will . . . punish you, *all* of you, if you don't . . . obey them.'

'Victor,' Deacon said urgently, 'please, *listen* to me. *Trust* me. I'll do everything I can to help you. I give you my word. All I ask is that we leave this place, now, just the three of us. We'll — '

'*No!*' snarled Victor, suddenly tearing the hammer from his belt again and raising it high overhead. 'No! The bats are my first . . . responsibility. And you *will* h-help us, you, your police force, your government, whoever. Sooner or . . . later, you'll realise you have . . . no *choice!*'

Into the heavy silence that followed his outburst he continued earnestly, 'Christopher . . . you can't even . . . *begin* to imagine the power these bats possess!

Even now they're . . . communicating their . . . orders to the lower species, filling their heads with images, as they filled *my* head with them! B-but this time their message is *simple*, Christopher! It is simply . . . to *kill!* To kill the *humans!*'

Deacon shook his head again. 'They're not doing anything of the sort, Victor. They *can't*. It's all in your mind.'

Victor raised the hammer again. 'Can't you s-see I'm trying to *help* you?' he asked, tears returning to his black eyes. 'I don't want this to happen! And it doesn't *h-have* to! But it *will*, Christopher, unless they're . . . taken home. Th-that's all they're asking for.'

He swayed a little, let the arm holding the hammer drop back to his side, and then slumped, exhausted, against the massive pipe again.

'They can and *will* raise an army, if they have to,' he murmured. 'C-close to twenty different species of bat, numbered in the t-tens of th-thousands. M-more than five hundred feral boars and f-four thousand wildcats. A quarter of a million foxes. Sixty-five million rats. And in time, wh-who knows? P-perhaps . . . even Man himself.'

He fell silent again. Overhead, batwings fluttered restlessly. Deacon's eyes found those of his wife. He could see that she, like he, wanted nothing more than to dismiss what Victor had said as the ravings of a madman. But what if they *weren't?* Could they really take that chance and call Victor's bluff?

For the time being, at least, Deacon felt it was safer to humour him. 'It's not a decision I can make on my own,' he said carefully. 'I'd need to speak with the authorities. Tell them what you've told me. After that, what happens would be up to them.'

Victor considered that for a moment, then raised his eyes to the shadowy ceiling and said softly, '*Bem, meinos pequenos?*'

He waited a moment, his dark, turned-down lips working faintly and in silence. Then, as if to some unheard question, he nodded again. '*Sim, podemos confiar sua palavra,*' he whispered.

Another long moment passed, as he stared off into the darkness above them. Then he turned his attention back to

Deacon and Jan and said, 'Y-you will tell them . . . they have no choice.'

Deacon felt a fleeting moment of relief, that he and Jan were going to get out of this after all. 'All right, Victor. We'll tell them.'

'*You* will . . . tell them,' Victor corrected. '*She* will stay here.'

Deacon felt the blood drain from his face, heard Jan utter a breathless, '*No!*'

'Victor, I'm not leaving here on my own. You have to let us go, *both* of us, if only as a sign of goodwill!'

Victor shook his head. 'No. She . . . stays. And if your government refuses to obey . . . then sh-she becomes the first casualty of the war that is . . . bound to follow.'

'Victor . . . '

Victor said, 'It is not my choice,' and threw another glance overhead. 'It is theirs. And I *obey* them.'

'For the love of *God*, Victor . . . ' Deacon began, but could see that there would be no dissuading him. In desperation he said, 'All right. You need a hostage. I understand that. *I'll* stay!'

'Chris . . . '

Ignoring Jan, Deacon went on as persuasively as he could, 'Let Jan go. *Please*. I mean, it doesn't make any real difference, does it? You've still got a hostage. You've still got a messenger!'

Victor looked into his face, searching his eyes, and the look of sadness in him became more pronounced. Perhaps he was remembering the many evenings they'd spent together at *Sombrieul*, the conversation and laughter and warmth and hospitality he'd been shown before things had changed, before *he* had changed.

Abruptly he nodded. 'Yes. She will go.'

Again Jan said, 'Chris — '

He took her by the arms. In the torchlight the tears on her cheeks glistened like quicksilver. 'Go,' he said. 'Tell Sears. Tell him *everything*. And when he's decided what he's going to do, tell him to call me.' He glanced quickly at Victor. 'Is that all right, Victor? That the authorities can contact me on my mobile?'

Victor nodded.

Turning back to Jan, he thrust the flashlight into her hands. 'I'll be all right,' he said. 'Victor won't let any harm come to me.'

Yet, he added silently.

Unable to speak at all now, Jan could only pull him close, press her lips to the side of his face, squeeze him and hope that the pressure could in some way convey the true depth of her love for him. Deacon, feeling hollow, squeezed her in return, kissed her hair, whispered, '*Go*.'

She took some coaxing, but at last he broke their embrace and led her to the door, where Victor turned the wheel and pushed it open to reveal the stinking darkness of the sewer beyond. Jan looked into Deacon's face, her eyes liquid, her lips twitching uncontrollably. Deacon just nodded and tried to tell her by his expression, *It'll all be okay.*

Catching his eye, Victor husked, 'You will wait here. You w-will not attempt to leave. If you do, they will kill you.'

Deacon, all too aware of the soft but persistent fluttering above him, nodded.

Then Jan was gone, Victor was gone,

and Deacon was plunged into impenetrable darkness, feeling sick to his stomach, and praying to God that the bats wouldn't try to invade *his* mind, as they had invaded Victor's.

14

'Well,' said Assistant Commissioner Alec Parnis, 'I think we can safely say that we've never had to deal with a situation quite like *this* one before.'

A tall man in his early fifties, with a thick waist, short, black-fading-to-grey hair and a constant five o'clock shadow, he regarded the group assembled around the table before him through troubled brown eyes. It was a little before eleven o'clock on Tuesday morning, and they were gathered in Eggerton Central's No 1 Briefing Room.

Present were Sears and Ryan; DCI Richard Palmer; Dr Josephine Lloyd, an American psychiatrist whom the police often called upon to evaluate psychiatric and pathological cases; DI Harry Crown, one of the Constabulary's most skilled hostage negotiators; and, from the Armed Response Unit, Specialist Firearms Officer Sergeant Steve Lowe.

The only stranger among them was a stocky, short-haired man who sat quietly at the far end of the table. He was a muscular thirty year-old with a clean-shaven, clearly-defined jaw, high cheekbones and dark, very slow-to-blink eyes. He wore a beige shirt with silver collar pins, light-weight brown trousers notched tight at the waist by a silver-buckled, royal blue stable belt, and low-ankle combat boots. On the table beside him sat a beige beret which bore an insignia depicting Excalibur in flames.

Earlier, the Assistant Commissioner had introduced him as Major Peter Fletcher, commander of C Squadron, 42 SAS.

Sears, seated to one side of the Assistant Commissioner, pinched at the tired flesh between his eyes. A long, busy morning had followed an even longer, busier night. No sooner had he arrived home and dropped into bed than the ringing of the phone had jarred him from his usual piecemeal, troubled sleep, and almost before he realised it, there was Ryan at the other end, saying something about Deacon's wife turning up at a police station in C-Division, looking like a half-drowned rat and in a severe state of shock.

By the time he met Ryan there, a police doctor had given her a mild sedative, and she was looking a little less wild-eyed than when she'd first stumbled in off the street. She'd still looked pretty rough, though, her fine, fair hair bedraggled, her make-up smudged, her skin pale and chilled, like marble. She'd been given a change of clothes that were a little on the large side, but the best C-Division had been able to muster at such short notice. According to the Station Reception Officer, the clothes she'd been wearing when she'd first come in had been soaking wet, and so had she.

Piece by piece, Sears had managed to coax everything from her; how she'd been abducted from her own home by Victor Santoro, how Santoro had used her to lure Deacon to the sewer in which he and the bats were hiding, about the story Santoro had told them, and of his demands.

He'd taken a lot of it with a pinch of salt, of course. Santoro's appearance, for example. In the poor light he'd probably looked worse than he actually was, as indeed *anyone* would, if they'd been living as rough as the Brazilian had, for as *long* as he had. As for the story he'd had to tell . . . well, they'd already established that the man was a PQMS.

Still, Santoro's altered appearance certainly tied in with those puzzling DNA results. And Sears reminded himself that Janet Deacon was a doctor, highly skilled, highly intelligent and not likely to let her imagination run away with her in any circumstances.

While Jan repeated everything for the official statement, Sears asked for and was given the use of an empty office, where he called Deacon's mobile. It was answered almost immediately.

'Yes?'

Deacon's voice sounded edgy, breathless, like that of a man struggling to hold onto his nerve. There was a faint echo behind it.

'Hello, Doc. It's me, Sears.'

'Yes, yes. What about Jan? Is she — ?'

'She's all right, Doc. But she had a pretty wild story to tell.'

Silence.

'Is he there with you now?' asked Sears.

'Yes.'

'Your wife says he's . . . *changed*.'

After another brief hesitation, Deacon said carefully, 'Yes.'

'She says he's somehow developed certain batlike, uh, *characteristics*. That can't be right, can it?'

'I wouldn't have said so,' Deacon replied. 'But he *has*.'

'Well, listen. I'm going to get you out of there, but it may take a while. Do you think you're safe enough for the time being?'

'I think so.'

'Good. Will he speak to me?'

'I'll ask.'

He heard Deacon shift the phone, say something. Then there came a second voice, a little further away than the first, with a short, guttural quality to it. A moment later Deacon said, 'No. He's said all he's going to say.'

'All right, we'll let it go for now. But I'm working on it, Doc. Trust me.'

He rang off. It was late, and he was starting a headache. But how was Deacon feeling about now, trapped in near-total darkness with a maniac and a bunch of disease-ridden bats for company? A bloody sight worse, most probably.

He sat there for a few moments, just thinking, then went out to the main desk and asked if there was any chance of a cup of coffee, milk, no sugar. The SRO told him there was *every* chance, so Sears went back into the empty office and started making phone calls until it arrived.

Now, mid-way through the following morning, the Assistant Commissioner said, 'Santoro's demands are ludicrous, of course. There's no way we can agree to them.'

'No,' agreed Sears. 'But we need to keep him in promise-land until we decide what we *are* going to do. And we need to make our decision as quickly as possible, because from what Janet Deacon told us, he's already on a pretty short fuse.'

The Assistant Commissioner nodded. 'What response have we had from the Health Protection Agency?'

'They've confirmed that John Cooper died from a previously unknown strain of Ebola, which they're tentatively calling Ebola *Brasilia*.'

'Which means that these bats have *got* to be eradicated,' said the Assistant Commissioner. He turned to Harry Crown. Crown was an average-looking man with a smooth, kind face that made him perfect for hostage negotiation. His was a face you instinctively felt you could trust, with soft lines and gentle grey eyes. 'Do you think we can still talk Santoro down, Harry?'

Crown considered his answer before he gave it. 'It would have been easier in the initial period, before things went this far,' he opined. 'Now we're going to meet a lot of resistance. A *lot* of it.'

Dr Lloyd agreed. She was a stunningly attractive ex-pat in her middle thirties, with well-spaced hazel eyes but a rather sober manner. 'By now this man will be battling strong emotions, a feeling of ambivalence, a fear of losing control,' she added. 'Any attempt to reason with him now will only increase the feeling that everything's getting away from him. It could make him lose what little restraint he has left and do something . . . ' she searched for the right word and finally settled on, ' . . . *spectacular.*'

'You mean kill Deacon?' prodded the Assistant Commissioner.

'Kill Deacon. And potentially set those bats loose.'

'That's my feeling, too,' admitted the Assistant Commissioner. 'And if the way John Cooper died is any indicator, the consequences of setting those bats loose hardly bear consideration.'

His eyes dropped to the copy of Jan's statement, which was on the top of the pile of reports and diagrams in front of him. The relevant paperwork had been copied for each of them and sat before them all now. 'I'm reluctant to sanction a tactical assault,' he said, 'but I don't really see any option. Any ideas?'

Steve Lowe, the Specialist Firearms Officer from Eggerton's Armed Response

Unit, said, 'If we could coax the target out into the open and guarantee a clear shot, I'd say we risk it. But even if we take down Santoro, that still leaves the bats — potentially the greater threat. In the circumstances, I think that makes it a job for the army.'

The Assistant Commissioner looked at Major Fletcher. The SAS man had arrived before anyone else, and by prior arrangement had entered the building quickly and quietly by means of a fire exit. He hadn't moved throughout the entire briefing, but now finally shifted slightly in his chair and, unfolding a plan from the paperwork in front of him, said briskly, 'This is the room in which the hostage is being held, am I right?'

Sears and the others unfolded their own copies. 'Yes,' said Sears. 'It's what they call a pipe subway. They regularly divert the flow of water through the pipes in these rooms and redirect it to any number of rivers and waterways elsewhere. In that way they avoid the risk of the sewers themselves overflowing.'

'As you can see, there's a door at either

end. This one, leading in from the sewer itself, is unlocked. You enter by turning a wheel in the centre of the door that releases two bolts on the other side.'

'And the door is made of . . . ?'

'Cast iron, four inches thick.'

'It opens inwards or outwards?'

'Outwards.'

'All right. Go on.'

'You can only gain access to the door at the far end from a tunnel connected to the pumping station about half a mile away, but it's padlocked on the outside.'

'And that opens outwards as well?'

'Yes.'

Fletcher studied the plan some more, his dark eyes scouring the page. 'Speed is going to be crucial on this,' he muttered. He was very well spoken, from one of the country's better families, Sears thought. 'So we can't afford to be held up by padlocks. And if these bats have the acute hearing Dr Deacon's statement seems to imply, they might hear us before we can get in, no matter how quiet we try to be.'

'You'll have to use the other door, then,' said Sears. 'Enter the room by way of the sewer itself.'

'Yes. But even that'll be chancy. We have to turn the wheel before we can open it. That'll slow us down, too — *and* forewarn Santoro.'

'But if you can get inside quickly enough?' pressed the Assistant Commissioner.

Fletcher said flatly, 'We use a four-man squad, myself and three other ranks, and we go in behind an M84 stun grenade. While this disorientates Santoro and his bats, one of my men extracts Deacon. The other two hit the bats with propane-filled flamethrowers. Propane will be cleaner and safer than liquid fuel, and just as effective. The only difference will be less smoke and less chance of fuel spattering everywhere.'

'And Santoro?' asked the Assistant Commissioner.

'If we can take him alive, we will,' replied the major. 'But I can't make any promises. If he's as dangerous as you seem to think he is, and I have reason to believe that he poses a threat to my men or myself, I'll kill him.'

It went very quiet around the table.

'There *is* another possibility,' said Sergeant Lowe. 'If, as I say, we can somehow coax Santoro out into the open, my men could take him down. No need to kill him, just incapacitate him. That could simplify your part a bit, Major. At least you wouldn't have Santoro to worry about.'

'But what if Santoro *is* in some kind of telepathic contact with the bats, as Dr Deacon suggests?' Sears argued. 'If they sense that he's been harmed — or even if they simply hear the shot that cuts him down and work it out from that — they'll go crazy. What happens to Deacon *then?*'

'Jack,' said DCI Palmer, speaking for the first time, 'you know as well as I do that there's no mental link between Santoro and these bats.'

'With respect, sir, I don't know any such thing,' Sears replied bluntly. 'Not for certain. None of us does.'

He put his elbows on the table. 'According to Janet Deacon, Santoro made a very specific threat last night. As ridiculous as it sounds, he claimed that these bats of his were going to somehow invade the minds of other mammals and turn them against us. So I had DS Ryan here do some checking overnight. Tell 'em what you found, Frank.'

Ryan glanced around the table, then consulted the folder he'd been clutching all through the meeting. 'I rang all the zoos, animal sanctuaries and council offices within a thirty-mile radius,' he reported. 'Four out of six zoos reported unusual or uncharacteristic activity among some of their animals — restlessness, aggression, in-fighting, an almost desperate desire to escape captivity. It was the same story with the animal sanctuaries.'

'I've also found fifteen separate reports of foxes attacking dogs, ponies and livestock overnight, which is more or less unheard-of. And two council clean-up crews working the markets in C-Division early this morning had to abandon the job and get out quickly because the streets were suddenly crawling with rats — rats that actually *chased* them back to their trucks. And *this*,' he concluded, 'after a reported *decrease* in the local rat population.'

Sears glanced at his colleagues. 'As fantastic as it sounds, I don't think we can afford to dismiss all this as coincidence. Something definitely stirred those animals up last night. Was it Santoro's bats? Your guess is as good as mine. But I do think we have to at least acknowledge the possibility.'

'Even if we acknowledge it,' said the Assistant Commissioner, 'it doesn't really alter things a great deal. We still need to rescue Deacon and ensure that those bats are destroyed or contained before they get the chance to escape.'

'All right,' said Sears. 'So we stick with Major Fletcher's plan. But with one modification.'

All eyes turned to him. Fletcher said, 'Which is . . . ?'

'I'll go in ahead of your mob,' said Sears, continuing quickly, 'I'll tell Santoro that I'm representing the government, which of course I *am*, and that I want to assure myself that everything really *is* as it's been reported to us, and that Deacon's still in good health, before I commit us to any cooperation. It shouldn't be too difficult to convince him. According to Janet Deacon, Santoro's thinking has been severely impaired over the past few months. I'll get him to take me down into this pipe subway, and when we get inside, I'll distract him in some way and leave the door unlocked. That should save you a few vital seconds, Major.'

DCI Palmer said, 'I'm sorry, Jack, but I can't allow that.'

'It's a good idea, though,' said Fletcher. 'Maybe I'll have one of my men do it. He works it so that he leaves the door unlocked, and makes sure Deacon is in exactly the right spot when all hell breaks loose. His priority then is to get Deacon out just after the rest of my squad go in with the flamethrowers.'

'*I'll* do it,' Sears insisted, throwing a glance at the Assistant Commissioner. 'It's my case, sir, and I want to see it through to the end.'

'And earn yourself a George Medal in the process?' asked Palmer, sarcastically.

Ignoring that, Sears turned his attention back to the SAS man. 'I can do it.

You just tell me where you want us to be when you come storming in, Major, and I'll make sure we're there.'

The Assistant Commissioner was silent for a while as he considered the plan, the risks, the inevitable accusations of heavy-handedness if it all went wrong, the potential threat to the population at large if the bats were somehow allowed to escape. At the moment they were trapped in one place. They might never get a better opportunity to deal with them once and for all.

Naturally he would have to discuss the matter with the Commissioner and the Deputy Commissioner first, and they in turn would have to confer with the Home Office. But in principal, he wouldn't see any other option.

Quietly he said, 'Thank you, everyone. Now, if you'll excuse me, I have some calls to make. But in principle at least, I believe we have our plan.'

15

Two treacle-slow hours later, Sears received a phone call asking him to come along to the Assistant Commissioner's office. When he got there, he found that the Assistant Commissioner had already been joined by DCI Palmer and DI Crown.

As he took a seat, the Assistant Commissioner said, 'I've just received a call from the Home Office, Jack. In the circumstances, we've been told to proceed as we see fit.'

Sears nodded. He knew what was coming now. The Assistant Commissioner would want to make absolutely sure that he was still willing to go through with this, and that he hadn't just volunteered on the spur of the moment, or out of some misguided sense of duty.

He listened as patiently as possible to all the arguments, knowing he now had a good opportunity to change his mind, or at least allow the AC and Palmer change it for him, but he didn't.

As much as anything else, he felt he owed it Deacon, whom he'd dragged into this business in the first place. But more than that, if this all went according to plan, there was always the chance that Charlie would read about it afterwards and admit, albeit grudgingly, that the police — and just maybe her old man — had their uses after all.

When he saw that Sears' mind was made up, the Assistant Commissioner suggested that they discuss strategy. Sears forced himself to focus as Harry Crown advised him on how he should deal with the situation in general and Santoro in particular. That done, and with assurances from Palmer that he would have back-up all the way, Sears finally used the speakerphone on the Assistant Commissioner's desk to call Deacon's mobile number.

'Hello? Yes?'

Deacon's voice sounded tinny and urgent as it filled the office.

'It's me, Doc. It's all been arranged.

We're getting you out of there.'

Deacon gave an audible swallow. 'How? When?'

'That's what I have to sort out with your friend, there,' said Sears. 'Put him on, will you?'

'I don't think he — '

'Just put him on,' snapped Sears.

He listened while Deacon said something to his captor. He had a mental image of that dark pipe subway, lit only by the feeble white-blue glow of Deacon's mobile phone, of the soft, sinister fluttering sounds echoing hollowly in the shadows overhead, and realised he was going to experience all that for himself very, very soon.

Suddenly a new voice said softly, 'Yesss . . . '

It made Sears' mouth dry up just to hear it. He looked from the AC to Palmer, from Palmer to Crown. Then, clearing his throat, he said as authoritatively as he could manage, 'Victor Santoro?'

' . . . yes . . . '

'My name is Sears, Detective Inspector

Jack Sears, Eggerton CID. I've just been discussing your, ah, demands with my superiors.'

There was a long pause. Then Santoro said, ' . . . and . . . ?'

Sears drew another breath. 'We're prepared to see that you get every cooperation,' he replied, lying through his teeth. 'But before we commit ourselves, I need to see *you*, and Deacon, for myself.'

'*No!*' rasped the half-voice at the other end of the connection.

'*Yes,*' insisted Sears, continuing forcefully, 'And I'll tell you why, Professor. Deacon's wife has told us a pretty fantastic story, and frankly, you can't blame us for not believing it. But there's a man's life at stake here, so we're prepared to give you the benefit of the doubt, so long as we meet, you and I, and I can confirm for myself that everything she's told us is true. Once I've satisfied myself about that, and the wellbeing of Dr Deacon himself . . . *then* we can talk.'

'You can't . . . t-trick me . . . ' chafed Santoro.

'Do you think I'd dare?' countered

Sears. 'You're holding all the aces, Professor. You've got the hostage. You've got the bats. And you've got everything to gain by cooperating with me. In any case, what have you got to lose? If I was foolish enough to try and trick you, your bats would kill me, wouldn't they?'

'Yes,' rasped Santoro.

'And if they didn't,' Sears went on, 'you'd end up with two hostages instead of one.'

He paused a moment, to let that sink in.

'It's heads you win, tails you can't lose, Professor,' he said persuasively. 'So what's it to be?'

He heard the other man move the phone, heard a muffled exchange with Deacon. Then: 'V-very . . . well. Chris . . . topher says you c-can be . . . trusted. You come. B-but y-you come . . . alone. A-and no . . . tricks.'

'No tricks,' agreed Sears. His eyes locked with those of the Assistant Commissioner as he said, 'Shall I come now?'

'N-no!' Santoro replied hurriedly. 'No . . .

n-not in . . . daylight. Tonight, after dark.' And he added softly, 'The d-dark is . . . *our* time.'

'All right,' said Sears. 'Shall we say ten o'clock?'

He took Santoro's silence to mean agreement.

'Ten o'clock it is, then,' he said. 'But just let me remind you, Professor. If you do anything to harm Dr Deacon, or anything to turn those bats of yours loose, then it's over. You'll get no help from the British Government, no help from *anyone*. Do I make myself clear?'

Again Santoro made no reply. For a moment Sears was afraid that he'd rung off. But then the breathless, struggling voice at the other end said, 'C-come at ten. We will . . . await you.'

Sears shivered.

★   ★   ★

The call made, he returned to his own office, where Ryan, unasked, fetched him a coffee. Clearly the word had already gone out that the plan was a goer. The tall

Detective Sergeant lingered as he set the mug down on Sears' desk and after another moment said impulsively, 'Mind if I say something, Guv?'

'Knock yourself out,' invited Sears.

'I think you want your bloody head tested,' Ryan said with feeling.

Sears quirked a humourless smile. 'Thank you for the vote of confidence.'

Having got that off his chest, Ryan went out and closed the door behind him, leaving Sears to stare moodily at the steam coming off the surface of the coffee.

After another moment he reached a decision and picked up the phone. He punched in a number, his lips drawing tight as he waited none-too-patiently for the call to be answered.

After a few seconds, a voice at the other end said, 'Hello?'

Sears said cautiously, 'Hello, Steph, it's me.'

There was a pause at the other end of the line. Then he heard Stephanie's voice say, '*Jack?*'

'Jack,' he said. 'I just thought I'd give

you a call. You know, see how life's been treating you.'

Her voice betrayed her surprise. 'I'm fine,' she said. 'Fine. And you?'

'Oh, you know. Same old same old.'

The line hissed with an uncomfortable silence.

'How's Charlie?' he asked.

'Oh, she's okay. Busy as ever, of course.'

'With that civil liberties group of hers, I suppose?'

'Yes.'

'And young Andrew?'

Now her voice seemed to come alive. 'Oh, you should see him, Jack. He's a real live-wire. Into everything.'

'They always are at that age,' he commented.

Inwardly, however, he was calling himself all the silly buggers under the sun, because now that he'd finally made the call he'd been wanting to make for so long, he couldn't think of a single thing to say.

Groping around, he finally settled on, 'I'm not interrupting anything, am I?'

'Well . . . '

'If I *am*, I'll go.'

'No, no. I can spare you a few minutes,' she replied. 'Was there, uh, any particular reason for calling, Jack?'

'Not really,' he said. Then, on impulse, he added, 'Well, actually, yes, there *was*.' He closed his eyes and said, as levelly as he could manage, 'I just wanted to make sure you're *happy* now, Steph. You know, now that we're not together anymore.'

She was quiet for a moment. At length she said, 'That's a funny thing to say.'

'*Are* you happy?' he pursued. 'Was it the right thing to do, do you think? To split up?'

He could sense that she wanted to say *yes*, but didn't want to hurt his feelings. 'Do *you* think it was the right thing to do?' she countered.

'You *know* what I think,' he said gruffly.

She sighed. 'Jack,' she said. 'Is everything all right? You sound a bit strange.'

'I'm fine.'

'Have you been drinking?'

'On duty? Never,' he replied. 'I suppose

I just wanted . . . you know . . . to tell you.'

'Tell me what?'

He experienced another moment of unreality as he finally said, 'That I still love you.'

There was complete silence at the other end of the line. Then she said, 'Well, there's a first. You've never told me *that* before.'

'I didn't think I had to.'

'It might have helped, you know.' Again she said, 'Jack, are you *sure* you're all right?'

'Yes.'

'But you'd tell me if anything was wrong, wouldn't you?'

''Course I would.'

It occurred to him suddenly that this had been a very bad idea. He didn't really know what he'd been expecting her to say. He'd been hoping she'd say that she loved him too, and was as sick of living on her own as he probably was, and what if we get together again, you know, like a date, and see how things develop from there?

But she didn't say any of those things. All she'd said was, *Well, there's a first.* And she was absolutely right.

He understood then that, as far as she was concerned, it really *was* over between them.

'Look,' he said suddenly, sitting forward, 'I've got to go. But I meant it, Steph.'

She said, 'I know you did, Jack.'

'Remember me to Charlie,' he went on, speaking hurriedly now. 'I know we haven't always seen eye to eye, but . . . I love her, too. And the little one.'

'Jack — '

'Look after yourself, Steph,' he said, and hung up.

The phone rang again almost immediately, jarring him. He snatched it up, said, 'Sears.'

'Major Fletcher, here, Detective Inspector. I wonder if I could come up and see you? We need to discuss what's going to happen tonight.'

Sears nodded. 'Come as soon as you like,' he muttered. 'I've got nothing better to do.'

★ ★ ★

Sears arrived at Fenady Street a little before ten o'clock, parked the Audi in front of Deacon's Auris and then flashed his headlights twice. After he switched off the ignition, it grew very quiet in the car. He opened the door, climbed out into the warm night and closed the door softly behind him. Above him, the sky was a purple velvet cloth strewn with diamonds.

Flexing his fingers around the flashlight in his left hand, he glanced to left and right and behind him. There was no sign of life anywhere. But he knew that this street would fill quickly and quietly as soon as he and Santoro entered the sewer. Armed Response Officers, uniformed coppers, Incident Support Units and more — they'd all move into position with ghostly silence and then begin the hardest job of all — waiting to see exactly how this thing turned out.

He shone his flashlight up over the tall, decaying buildings to left and right, wondering if he was going to find the bats themselves waiting for him. He hoped not. He wanted those murderous little bastards trapped below ground, where Fletcher's squad could deal with them once and for all.

Seeing nothing, he started to walk slowly up the street, his footsteps curiously muted by the waterproof fishing boots he'd been given to wear.

The night was sticky, humid. He felt uncomfortable in his grey suit and blue tie. He thought maybe this wasn't such a good idea after all, putting himself through this just to prove a point to Charlie.

Then, without warning, a shadow detached itself from a corner sixty metres ahead, and he broke stride. Suddenly he felt even more vulnerable than he had before, because if Janet Deacon was to be believed — and he saw no reason why she shouldn't be — then Santoro could see him as clear as day, while all he could make out of the other man was a small, dark, hunched shape.

Clearing his throat, he called, 'Professor Santoro?'

His voice echoed along the deserted street.

The figure raised one arm and waved him forward.

Sears walked closer. Still Santoro remained a shadow among shadows. When no more than three or four metres separated them, he halted again. 'Professor Santoro?' he repeated, straining to see through the darkness.

The shadow said in a soft, sibilant voice, 'S-Sears?'

'I'm Sears.'

'A-and you came . . . alone?'

'I came alone.'

'Y-you will t-take the b-bats . . . home? M-me home?'

'Once I'm satisfied that everything you told the Deacons is true,' Sears replied. 'And that Dr Deacon himself is unharmed.'

'He is.'

'I need to see that for myself,' said Sears.

The shadow bobbed the head that sat low on its narrow shoulders. 'You . . . will. B-but n-no . . . tricks. They w-will kill you if you t-try to trick them. They will . . . or *I* will . . . '

The shadow stirred, the right arm came up, and moonlight slithered off the matted head of a hammer. *The* hammer.

Sears swallowed softly. 'I think there's been enough killing, don't you?' he asked quietly. Then: 'Shall we just get on with it?'

Putting the hammer back into his belt, the shadow gestured that he should come forward. He did so. Santoro indicated that he should enter the alleyway beyond the half-open gate. As he walked past the shadow to do so, he got a brief, unpleasant smell of the man. Santoro stunk of rottenness and neglect, of faeces and old blood and death.

Santoro followed him through the gate and pushed it shut behind him. It closed with a protesting squeal that sounded over-loud in the otherwise pristine silence. Then he rasped, 'Wait. F-face the w-wall.'

'What?'

'F-face the wall.'

Knowing better than to argue about it, Sears reluctantly did as he was told, then waited while Santoro shuffled closer and clumsily patted him down, doubtless searching for a hidden weapon, or maybe a wire.

He found neither.

'G-go,' Santoro said at last, stepping back and gesturing again toward the end of the alleyway.

'Can I use my flashlight now?' asked Sears.

' . . . y-yes . . . '

Switching the flashlight on, he made a brief inspection of the mean-looking passage and then started down toward the open manhole at its far end, the blood starting to throb sickeningly in his ears. At Santoro's bidding, he made a cautious descent into the sewer below.

Once underground, Santoro seemed to gain a little more confidence. They were in his world now, and they both knew it. 'G-go . . . ' the Brazilian ordered when they both stood knee-deep in sewage at the bottom of the old ladder. 'Th-that way.'

Sears waded through the filthy water, trying to take comfort from what he knew would be happening above ground right now. Incident Support Units would be sealing off the street, representatives of the Health Protection Agency would be donning bright orange biohazard gear, ready to isolate whoever came back out of the sewer once this was all over. Members of Steve Lowe's Armed Response Unit would be taking up positions at empty windows and lonely rooftops, with the AN/PVS-22 Universal Night Sights affixed to their Heckler & Koch 33SG1 sniper rifles trained unerringly on the shadow-filled alleyway.

And then, of course, would come Fletcher and his men, four bulky ghosts in camouflaged, charcoal-lined Mk IIIB NBC protection suits and Osprey body armour, each of its twenty-two pieces weighed down with heavy trauma plates. They would make one final check on the firing triggers, igniter triggers and safety catches of their modified M2A1-7 flame-throwers, and finally descend stealthily into the sewer.

'H-here . . .' chafed Santoro, and Sears realised with a start that they had reached the door to the pipe subway. 'O-open it . . .'

Mouth dry now, Sears climbed the five stone steps and grabbed the wheel, turned it. He felt the seals relax around the doorframe, tugged it open and shone his flashlight inside.

Deacon was slumped on a massive pipe about halfway down the left-side of the room. He raised his hands to shield his eyes from the light. Sears stepped inside and said, 'It's all right, Doc. I'm here now.'

Deacon slowly lowered his hands. He looked gaunt and hollow-eyed, and there was a shading of stubble across his jaw. He pushed up from the pipe against which he'd been leaning, made to approach Sears but then stopped as he heard a sudden, restless fluttering in the darkness above them. Sears heard it too, and shone the flashlight overhead.

Eyes blacker than jet glared down at him from pointed, feral faces.

He felt his heart run a little faster as he turned back to Santoro, getting his first half-way decent look at the scientist and thinking, *Oh Christ, he really is a fucking monster.*

Before Santoro could reach out and close the door behind him, Sears did it, trying to make the action look as natural as possible. Seeking to distract the man, he said, 'So, these are your bats, are they?'

As he had hoped, Santoro glanced briefly up into the darkness as Sears took his hands off the wheel without turning it.

The Brazilian whispered, 'N-no. I am th-their . . . *human*.'

Keeping the flashlight beam low now, Sears threw a look at Deacon and gestured toward the door with a quick flicker of his eyes. Deacon had been watching him all the while, saw that he had closed but not resealed the door and, swallowing, gave the smallest nod of acknowledgement.

Sears went a little closer to Deacon, but stopped short when he decided he'd reached the approximate position they needed to be in when Fletcher's squad made their move.

'Are you all right, Doc?' he asked, his voice echoing around the room. And when Deacon looked at him again, he tried to communicate with his expression that Deacon should come and join him.

Not entirely sure what was going on,

Deacon nevertheless cleared his throat and came nearer. 'I'm all right,' he said in a voice grown unaccustomed to speaking.

'And Professor Santoro hasn't harmed you?' asked Sears, playing for time and trying to keep things moving so that Santoro wouldn't have the opportunity to suspect a trap.

'I'm okay.'

'Good.'

Santoro shuffled a little closer. 'S-so. You h-have seen,' he whispered. 'N-now you will help?'

'I'd like to help *you*, Professor,' replied Sears. 'You clearly need it. Would you — ?'

Santoro shook his head irritably and took a backward step. 'Y-you will *help?*' he chafed. 'Y-you will t-take us h-home?'

Still playing for time, Sears said, 'I'll need to hear your story again, for myself.'

Santoro shook his head some more. He was rapidly losing what little patience he still possessed, and allowing an unpredictable anger to replace it. 'H-hurts . . . to talk!' he complained. Then, with a gesture towards Deacon, he breathed, '*He* will t-tell you!'

Sears turned to Deacon. 'All right. How about it, Doc?'

Deacon opened his mouth to reply.

And that was the moment the door flew back and someone — Fletcher, most probably — yelled, '*Incoming!*'

16

Even though Sears had been expecting it, the bellowed warning still paralysed him for vital fractions of a second.

Then something inside him took over, the instructions that Fletcher had given him earlier that day came rushing back, and he yelled to Deacon, '*Shut your eyes and cover your ears, NOW!*'

He dropped to a crouch and followed his own advice, burying his chin in his chest, covering his ears, almost forgetting to breathe in the electricity of the moment.

A split second later a black, hexagonal steel cylinder pocked with holes landed at the approximate centre of the floor, bounced, rolled and then went off.

The M84 stun grenade — known by the men who used it as a 'flash-bang' — almost immediately lived up to its name. There came a terrific flash of white light as its 4.5 grams of magnesium and potassium perchlorate combined to create a sudden burst of illumination equivalent to that of eight million candles. At the same time there came a tremendous, racketing boom of sound, one hundred and sixty decibels in volume, and the room seemed almost to shake with the force of it as its shock-wave spilled Sears, Deacon and Santoro to the floor.

Then chaos took over.

Startled bats began to flutter and dive everywhere, chirruping and chattering in a mixture of fear and fury. Daring to open his eyes after five agonising seconds, Sears clapped Deacon on the shoulder, and Deacon, still disorientated by the blast, struggled to rise just as the SAS squad burst into the room.

A tall, wide figure clutching a 9mm Heckler & Koch MP5A3 submachine gun came straight for them. Sears saw the SF-100 respirator attached to his M40 protective mask wobbling and realised that the soldier was shouting at him.

Sears yelled, '*Come on!*' and together he and Deacon stagger-ran toward the soldier.

By now the remainder of the squad had entered the room, two of them carrying the modified flame throwers on their backs. While the final man — Fletcher himself — slammed the door shut behind him and then began to cover them with his submachine gun, they flipped off the safety catches on their firing and igniter triggers and began to scour the ceiling with ten-metre streaks of flame.

Although the bats made difficult targets as they zipped and wheeled this way and that, ten or a dozen were engulfed almost immediately, and dropped to the ground in writhing, struggling puddles of fire.

Already recovering from the shock of the attack, however, the rest were even now taking evasive action, their shadows skittering madly across the ceiling above them.

Sears and Deacon had almost reached the soldier who was waving them on when one of the bats dived straight into the man's mask. The soldier jolted as the bat smashed head-first through one of the tinted eyepieces and bit into the eye beyond.

The soldier's respirator shuddered again to the sound of his scream and the finger inside his 7mm butyl-rubber glove tightened reflexively on the machine gun's trigger.

Reacting fast, Sears threw himself to the floor and pulled Deacon down with him as flame spat from the muzzle of the weapon and a deadly burst of 9mm bullets stitched into the far wall and sheered off the sewage pipes to ricochet in every direction.

As Sears made to rise again, another burning bat, this one still flapping and curling in on itself as it died, slapped to the concrete floor next to him.

In the next moment Santoro was there, shoving past him, throwing himself down beside the still-twitching trooper and tearing the machine gun from his hands. With a curse Sears went after him, leapt back when Santoro tried to use the weapon as a club and then threw himself flat again.

Santoro fired the machine gun and on the far side of the room Major Fletcher, like the rest of his men now trying to fight off a concerted attack from the surviving bats, dropped to his knees. He swung his own weapon around, stunned more than injured by the impact of the slugs because of his body armour, and was just about to return fire when Santoro fired the machine gun again and Fletcher's protective mask seemed to explode.

The major tumbled backwards in a crimson spray.

One of the two flamethrower men was hit by a bat that came at him from his blind side, whacked him in the shoulder and knocked him off-balance. The flame from his M2A1-7 went with him, white at its centre, a deep, deep orange at its outer edges, and swiped his companion across the chest, arm —

And across the propane-filled tank he wore on his back.

Suddenly the pipe subway lit up as bright as day and seemed to rock drunkenly as the tank exploded and shredded the man wearing it. Bats and their shadows flitted everywhere, still chattering and screeching, now maddened beyond reason.

The same burst of flame engulfed the final man, and Sears and Deacon saw him stagger as the wave of fire swallowed and then wholly consumed him, igniting his own tank. A second explosion rocked the room, throwing Santoro off his feet and sending the machine gun skittering from his misshapen fingers.

Knowing that they had to get out of there as soon as possible, Sears yelled 'Come on!' Still deafened himself, he doubted that Deacon could hear him, but he would certainly get the message.

With the stink of burning flesh and melting rubber clogging their throats and nostrils, Sears began to lead the way toward the closed door, but neither the bats nor Santoro were about to let them go without a fight.

All at once the infuriated bats were everywhere, fluttering around their heads, hurling themselves at the fleeing humans with all the strength they possessed.

And then there was Santoro, back on his feet again, his dark lips wrenched down in a scream of pure hatred, the MP5A3 once again in his claw-like hands and pointed their way.

Sears snatched at the weapon, ripped it from Santoro's grip, buried the collapsible stock into his right hip and pulled the trigger, expecting to seal the Brazilian's fate once and for all.

Nothing happened.

The machine gun was empty.

Santoro, still screaming at the top of his lungs, tore the hammer from his belt and came forward at a run. Sears yelled something himself, brought the machine gun around in an arc that clipped the half-man on the chin and sent him sprawling to the floor, spitting blood.

'*Go, go, go!*' yelled Sears.

They began to stagger-run again, each man cursing the disorientating effects of the stun grenade, but gradually the door came closer, closer —

And so did the bats.

Sears punched them aside, kept going. Deacon followed suit, his mind a riot of thoughts and half-thoughts and a tiny, insistent voice that kept repeating urgently, *Go, go, go . . .*

At last they reached the door — and

that was where Sears stopped, breathing hard.

Deacon, his face blackened and slick with sweat, came around to face him. '*Come on!*' he cried, grabbing for the door.

But Sears looked back at the confusion behind them, at the circling bats now flapping blindly into walls, at Santoro clawing groggily back to his hands and knees, and snarled grimly, 'I've got a better idea. If we can't fry the bastards, maybe we can *drown* 'em.'

Deacon couldn't believe what he was hearing. Grabbing Sears by the shoulder, he yelled, '*Forget it! We've got to get* out *of here!*'

In the uncertain flicker of the flames, Sears looked curiously at peace. '*You* have,' he said, and slowly brought his left hand up.

Deacon thought, *Oh my God.*

Blood was dripping from three separate bites on the back of the policeman's hand, just above the knuckles.

'Better get out of here,' Sears told him.

Deacon thought of John Cooper's flushed face, of the vomit leaking from his slack mouth. John Cooper, bleeding from his eyes and nose, his mouth and anus, John Cooper, dead within twelve hours.

'Not without you,' he said stubbornly.

'*Go!*' Sears shouted.

Deacon felt helpless, and sick because of it. He was torn by the desire to flee and reluctance to leave Sears to his fate. But what else could he do? Someone had to get out of this nightmare and tell the rest of the world what had happened.

He looked Sears in the face. Sears looked flushed and sweat-run, but he nodded.

'Thank you,' Deacon said, his voice a dry croak.

Sears nodded. 'Goodbye, Doc.'

Deacon pushed the door open, spilled out into the sewer beyond and shouldered the door shut behind him. There came a loud squeak as one of the bats was caught between the door and its seal. With a grunt, Deacon shouldered the heavy door shut, squashing the creature to a furry pulp.

Inside the room, Sears turned the wheel, sealing him in with Santoro and the surviving bats.

★ ★ ★

He turned and started walking back across the room, his stride deliberate now, his shoulders no longer hunched protectively but well and truly squared. The stale air stank of roasting flesh, and around him the walls, pipes and ceiling were scorched and fire-blackened. The only light came from the flames still feeding on the dead men.

Still down on his knees, Santoro watched him through eyes that were darker than the shadows in a closed coffin, wondering what came next.

Ignoring the bats that swooped at him, knowing they could do him no more harm than they already had, Sears knelt beside the soldier whose job it had been to extract them. He tore an egg-shaped grenade from the man's belt.

Santoro climbed to his feet, screamed, 'No!'

Ignoring him, Sears pulled the pin from the L2 grenade, shoved it down behind the largest of the pipes and then hurriedly backed away.

A little over four seconds later the grenade went off. It did its best to crush their eardrums and tear the room apart, but what its 170 grams of RDX/TNT actually did was precisely what Sears had been *hoping* it would do — it ruptured the main pipe so that dark, untreated water began to gush out across the body-littered floor.

The force of the blast had swatted both men over again. Now, as water continued to pour from the torn pipe, each pushed unsteadily back to his feet.

Sears made it first, planted himself in front of the door and clenched his fists. The blood from his left hand dripped steadily to cloud the water that was already starting to rise around his ankles. The bats fluttered lower, studying what was happening and trying to make sense of it.

Santoro hissed, 'S-step . . . aside.'

'Not a chance,' Sears replied. 'You're going to die down here, Professor. We *all* are.'

The bats were chattering furiously now, as understanding began to dawn. Santoro cocked his head, appearing for all the world to listen to them. Around them, the cascading water continued to splash and echo from the torn pipe, already near to calf-height.

Finally Santoro nodded, and dropping his gaze back to Sears, opened his mouth to articulate the bats' rage in a howl that bounced back off the scorched walls.

Then he threw himself forward, sending a wave of dirty water out ahead of him, and his hands came up, the fingers twisting into talons.

While the bats continued to swoop and flutter around his head, seeking to distract him and help Santoro finish him quickly, Sears brought up his fists.

Santoro came at him in a rush, shoved him backwards and then tried to punch him. But the scientist was just that — a scientist, not a fighter. The punch failed to connect.

Sears caught his balance, set himself again and threw a punch of his own. It caught Santoro on the jaw and whacked his head backward.

Wading through the rising water, Sears

hit him again, a left-right combination that then dropped to concentrate on the other man's stomach. Santoro kept howling, and now the howl contained rage and fear in equal measure.

Driven by his anger, Santoro surged forward again, smashed into Sears and carried him backward and down into the chill, foul-smelling water. The water closed over the policeman, he felt the concrete floor beneath his shoulder blades, the weight of Santoro pinning him there, the professor's dirt-encrusted fingers questing for and then finding his throat, closing ever tighter around it . . .

Sears twisted like an eel, trying to dislodge the other man, and all the while his lungs felt like they were going to explode. He reached out blindly, found Santoro's wrists more by accident than design, yanked hard and broke the stranglehold, and that was something, though by no means enough.

There was a near-frantic desperation in him now, as he continued to writhe and twist. Santoro had his hands full, trying to keep him below the surface, but the agitated circling of the bats overhead was distracting *him* too, and a momentary lapse in concentration finally gave Sears the chance to unseat him.

Santoro tumbled sideways, hit the water with a violent splash and went under. At the same moment Sears reared up from below, mouth open, chest heaving, and he thought with a kind of savage delight, *Now let's see how* you *like it*.

Even as Santoro started clawing his way back to the surface, Sears was on him, straddling him, one hand splayed across his contorted man-bat face.

As the water continued to rise and fill the room around them, and the bats continued to flap and flutter around his head and drag at his sodden hair and scratch at his face, he thought, *Die, you bastard! Die!*

But Santoro wasn't ready to die just yet. He struggled as hard as Sears had to throw off his opponent, but Sears wasn't having that, oh no.

Then Santoro's questing fingers closed around something hard. The hammer! He grasped the handle, brought the weapon up and rammed the claw-end deep into Sears' left shoulder.

Sears grunted. He didn't have enough breath to scream. But when Santoro dragged down on the wound, making the claw-end scrape against bone, the pain was so intense that a cry *did* escape him, and he thrust up, staggered back, leaving the hammer in Santoro's hand.

Santoro followed him up. The water was chest-high now. Sears' face twisted with a snarl and he half-fell forward, intending to finish it once and for all.

He never got the chance.

Santoro brought the hammer up in one swift movement. Droplets sprayed off the weapon in an arc of pearls.

Then he brought the hammer down right on the area immediately above Sears' left eye.

Sears went stiff, fell back, this time taking the firmly-embedded hammer with him. He vanished under the water's choppy surface, leaving only a lazy cloud of blood behind him.

Santoro swayed, sucked at the stink-filled air. He was exhausted, but still his mind was filled with the bats' ceaseless chattering, as they told him what to do: what he *must* do: what he had to do *now*.

Open the door, let them out..

He shifted awkwardly, for the water was pressing in on him now, making every movement sluggish and laboured, and as he did so, Sears' body bobbed back to the surface, face-up and slack, blood still billowing from his head wound.

The rising water had doused most of the flames by this time and the pipe subway was close to complete darkness again. Santoro looked at the body and felt a sudden wave of revulsion surge through him. According to Christopher, Sears had been a good man, a *decent* man. The kind of man *he* had once been.

Sears had only tried to do what he'd felt he *had* to do, what the bats had left him no *choice* but to do.

In no more than a handful of seconds he thought of everything that had happened since his own personal nightmare had begun, of every dirty thing he'd had to do, that the bats had *made* him do.

Then his mind filled with their

chattering again, desperate, demanding, chaotic, and screwing his face up, he clapped his hands to his ears and cried in his native Portuguese, *'All right! I'm doing it now!'*

He stumbled to the door, took hold of the wheel and began to turn it. At once the chattering inside his mind lessened. He was obeying orders. The bats were pleased.

He went to make another turn, but once again the unwelcome image of Sears' face came into his mind — the blank look which had dropped across it like a veil when the hammer had cracked his skull and pulped the frontal lobe.

He saw again the anger in Sears' eyes, the anger quickly replaced by sorrow and disappointment as some final, dying part of him realised that he'd failed in what he'd been trying to do here.

For what he'd been trying to do for the people he served.

Sensing his hesitation, the bats began to chatter again, faster, louder, ever more insistent.

Turn the wheel, turn the wheel . . .

And in that moment Professor Victor Santoro thought, *Yes, I'll turn the wheel*.

He turned it again, but this time the opposite way, sealing them all in.

That sent the bats back into a frenzy. Beside themselves with fury, some swooped down to skim over Santoro's distorted figure, others flew blindly into scorched walls or against the high, fire-darkened ceiling, searching for another means of escape.

And inside Santoro's head the chittering, chattering, clicking, squealing sound of his masters' voices rose to a mad crescendo, ordering him to turn the wheel, *demanding* it, threatening him with a million promises of pain if he didn't.

Santoro's face screwed tight. Again he covered his ears and tried to blot out the ceaseless cacophony. Again he failed.

The urge to do the bats' bidding was almost more than he could bear. But no. He had served them long enough as it was.

He refused.

Santoro believed it was the hardest thing he'd ever done. But he was wrong.

The hardest thing was to willingly sink down into the rising water and open his mouth so that it filled his lungs and silenced the fluttering forever.

★　★　★

The minute Deacon shoved his head through the manhole he was pinned by a spotlight and told to stay where he was. Within seconds the alleyway was filled with armed policemen in crackling orange biohazard suits and black body armour. Through these came other figures, scientists from the Health Protection Agency.

'Up you come,' said one of the armed policemen, 'Slowly, now.'

Deacon crawled out of the hole and was quickly helped to his feet.

'Dr Deacon, is it?' asked someone from the HPA.

Deacon nodded. He was starting to shiver.

'What happened?' asked one of the policemen.

Deacon shook his head. It was hard to

think, to organise his words.

'The bats, Doctor?' persisted the policeman.

'They're gone,' he said. 'Drowned.'

'Drowned?'

'There were soldiers,' he said. 'With flamethrowers. The bats killed them. Sears sealed himself in with the bats and drowned them instead.'

'They're dead, then?'

'Yes.'

'They're *all* dead?'

'Yes.'

'The soldiers? Sears?'

'*Yes, damn you!*'

One of the armed policemen was there again. 'All right, Doctor. It's all right now.'

Someone else demanded urgently, 'Did you receive any injuries, Doctor? Bites? Scratches?'

Deacon shook his head, but didn't expect them to take his word for it. They began to guide him out of the alleyway and into Fenady Street itself, which now seemed to be alive with Light-Alls and barriers and Incident Support Unit vans and people with weapons.

The feeling of confusion and disorientation came flooding back to him and his legs almost went out from beneath him. But then a sudden blur of movement over by the left-side barrier caught his attention, and suddenly he felt like crying. It was Jan, dipping beneath the barrier and making a run to reach him, and behind her, DS Ryan, moving swiftly, grabbing her arm to hold her back.

Deacon must have taken a step toward her without realising it, because a hand suddenly tightened on his shoulder and a voice said, 'All right, sir, just calm down now.'

He was too tired to resist much, anyway. Instead he looked at Jan from a distance of perhaps ten metres, read her lips as she asked, *Are you all right?*

He nodded. *I'm fine.*

Is it over?

I think so. I hope so.

That made her sag a little in Ryan's grasp. Ryan's face was also a picture of concern, and though he made no attempt to speak, his eyes asked the question.

Jack?

Deacon shook his head.

Ryan frowned, his eyes grew distant, then sharpened again. This time he did mouth a question. *Anyone?*

Again Deacon shook his head.

'Better come along now, Doctor. We need to get you checked over.'

Yes, Deacon thought hollowly. *Checked over and debriefed.*

He looked again at Jan, mouthed, *I'll see you soon.*

Jan smiled a tearful smile and mouthed, *I love you. You too.*

Then he allowed them to take him away.

★ ★ ★

Long minutes passed after that, and although Ryan waited as patiently as he could, in the hope that Deacon had been mistaken, no-one else came out of the manhole.

After a while Jan squeezed the tall sergeant's arm and he nodded sadly. Jack was gone. Fletcher's squad was gone. And so, he told himself, were Victor Santoro and his bats.

They were about to return to the barrier when they heard a sudden, restless fluttering in the night sky above.

Their heads snapped up, the breath caught in their throats . . . but then they relaxed, swapped a glance, a sheepish, relieved smile.

Because it was just the first of the pigeons, returning to the city.

THE END